BAD FOR YOU

International Bestselling Author

MONICA JAMES

Cover Model: Lawrence Templar
Photographer: Michelle Lancaster
Editing: Editing 4 Indies

Interior Design and Formatting by

TIPPETTS
E.M.

E.M. Tippetts Book Designs

Follow me on:
authormonicajames.com

OTHER BOOKS BY MONICA JAMES

ALL THE PRETTY THINGS TRILOGY

Bad Saint

Fallen Saint

Forever My Saint

The Devil's Crown-Part One (Spin-Off)

The Devil's Crown-Part Two (Spin-Off)

THE MONSTERS WITHIN DUET

Bullseye

Blowback

DELIVER US FROM EVIL TRILOGY

Thy Kingdom Come

Into Temptation

Deliver Us From Evil

IN LOVE AND WAR

North of the Stars

Fall of the Stars

REVENGE IS SWEET SERIES

Crybaby

HEART MEMORY TRANSFER DUET

Heart Sick

Love Sick

KISS OR KILL SERIES ·
Bad for You

STANDALONE
Mr. Write
Chase the Butterflies
Beyond the Roses
Someone Else's Shadow
Love Hard
Love Harder

CONTENT WARNING:

BAD FOR YOU is a **DARK ROMANCE** containing mature themes that might make some readers uncomfortable. It contains strong violence, sexual assault, trauma, child abuse, murder, profanity, drug use, criminal activity, blood gore, blood play, and some dark and disturbing scenes.

There is no cruelty to animals.

This twisted tale is not intended for the fainthearted.

PROLOGUE

"I've been a bad boy and need to be punished," says the *stronzo* tied to the bed in this shithole of a hotel.

His tiny dick is nowhere to be found under his disgusting belly, which jiggles as he cranes his thick neck to look at me standing at the foot of the bed. He licks his porty lips. I will take great pleasure in cutting out that tongue and feeding it to him.

I don't care what his name is.

I don't care what any of their names are.

It's not because I'm trying to detach myself from the deplorable acts I commit, but rather, I just don't care. It makes no difference to me. They're all a means to an end, and my endgame is survival because I am hunted.

An eye for an eye, the Bible says—the text my mother once lived by.

Once I found the woman who bore me for nine months, only to abandon me on the doorstep of Saint Maria's Orphanage, I thought an epiphany would strike and all would be healed.

What a naive fool I was.

I wish I could ask the simple question, *why*?

Wasn't I cute enough?

Did I cry too much?

Or could it be because I looked too much like *him?*

Many have said my mother and father's meeting wasn't fated in the stars. Rather, it was churned in the bowels of hell because nothing good would ever come from my mother, Sister Margarette, falling in love with the convicted and infamous serial killer, Patrick O'Loughlin, and having his daughter...me.

My mother was a woman of God, but she soon forgot the vows she took when her parish sent her to provide spiritual guidance to death row inmate #39280.

My father was found guilty of brutally raping and killing fifteen innocent women. For his sins, he was sentenced to death. During his time on death row, he apparently found God. I often wonder where God was when he tied Tina Gully to a radiator and starved her to death after he was done torturing her with a starved sewer rat.

Or was JC on a sabbatical when my father bludgeoned to death a nineteen-year-old French hitchhiker with his tire jack because he was having a bad day?

This man was my father, the man my mother fell in "love" with, but not before falling pregnant with the spawn of Satan—me.

I want to believe she saw some good in him. That she believed he could be saved. But I know the truth, and that truth is that my mother is as much a monster as my father once was.

The day he was executed was the day I was born.

Again, another cruel twist of fate because I always felt like a part of his soul took over mine on that day. That's the only explanation as to why I do the despicable things that I do and like them…so very much.

I'm not a bad person.

It's him, I reason with myself. It's his voice I hear, spurring his baby girl on to carry on with his legacy.

It can't be me because if it were, what does that say about who I am?

Oh, who am I kidding? There is no one to blame but me.

I lie because yes, I'm not a bad person. That's correct because I am far worse. I'm utterly ruthless and depraved and delight in all things blood and violence.

"You *have* been a very bad boy," I coo in a sickly sweet voice, which makes me want to vomit. But assholes like him eat this shit up. "So I'm going to punish you how you deserve."

The pile of shit on the bed giggles eagerly. Little does he know his time on this earth is about to be siphoned off in mere minutes.

The familiar swirl of euphoria stirs in my stomach, the excited feeling of all the bloody and macabre things coming this way.

I reason with myself that this *bastardo* deserves it. He's my enemy. He also dabbles in pimping out kids, so he deserves everything that's coming. He made his choice, and now, I make mine as I leap onto the bed, straddling him as I would a horse.

He likes it. But I'm going to like it even more when I scoop out his eyeballs and ram them down his throat.

I pinch his chin, pursing his lips out to resemble the little bitch that he is. "What's the worst thing you've ever done?"

He believes I'm getting off on his "bad boy" persona. "I've done so many bad things, baby, I'd make that pretty head of yours spin."

I gush dramatically. "Oh please, Daddy, tell me."

"I fuck up anyone who stands in my way…man, woman, or child. No one stops The D-Man from getting what he wants."

I barely contain my laughter. The D-Man? Dead man walking, perhaps?

"I heard you deal…drugs," I whisper, staging complete and

utter shock. "Is that true?"

"You heard right, baby. I'm the motherfucking king of these streets. People cower when they hear my name."

I smile, but nothing is sweet about it. "Is that because it's a fucking ridiculous name...Georgie Toole who wears SpongeBob pajamas to bed?"

I literally see the moment when The D-Man aka Georgie Toole realizes he's about to be fucked...and not in the way he paid me fifteen bucks for.

"Who are you?" He tugs at the cuffs around his wrists, but he isn't going anywhere. I made sure of that the moment I accidentally on purpose flushed the key down the toilet.

"I am no one," I reply because I am.

I don't know my name. I wasn't given one at birth. But the sisters at the orphanage named me Valentina because I was left on their doorstep on Valentine's Day. And it stuck.

But the woman who was more a mother to me than my own taught me to own that name. She taught me to be true to who I really am, and that is...I am a killer, trained by the woman who adopted me when I was ten years old.

And that woman is Gianna Ricci.

I owe her everything, which is why I do her bidding and do so with a smile.

"It's time to make your peace," I calmly state as I always do with the many faceless men like Georgie.

It's the least I can do.

"You fucking whore!" he screams, the cuffs rattling against the headboard. "I'm going to fucking kill you."

I tsk him lightly. "Shh, let us pray. Our Father, who art in heaven…"

Before he can pollute this world any further, I pull out the blade in my boot and stab him in the throat. I don't like delaying gratification.

"Hallowed be thy name," I continue, reciting the Lord's Prayer as my adopted Italian accent, thanks to Gianna, shines through.

This prayer was recited to me over and over as I was defiled, humiliated, and abused, so this is me taking it back as I won't allow the past to rule me.

His eyes widen, shock overcoming him as he realizes the mistake he made by picking up a "hooker" on the corner all because he wanted his dick sucked before reruns of *Seinfeld*.

I slice through Georgie's muscles and tendons with precision because I could do this with my eyes closed. I have been trained by the best. "Thy kingdom come, thy will be done."

Georgie's gurgles indicate he's drowning in his own blood. I imagine it's a horrible way to die, and the blood bubbles that pop from his mouth are almost hypnotic.

"On earth as it is in heaven," I continue, cutting across his throat, then slicing down his chest.

Blood coats my hands and face, just as it always does, and I can hear it—his heartbeat, as well as my father clapping in cadence to the beating of his failing heart.

"Give us this day our daily bread." I recite this prayer as it seems the appropriate thing to do when taking someone's life. But it also reminds me of why I do this and revel in the blood.

It reminds me of the blood that runs in my veins—part monster, part saint.

But I am beyond saving.

Once Georgie's chest is cut open, I peer into the cavity and am mesmerized by his heart—the epicenter of one's existence, the reason we do what we do. But as I crack open his rib cage, thanks to the tools I carry with me in my bag of tricks, I realize that even though I may have one of these, it doesn't feel how others do, and that's because I don't feel…a thing.

I'm as hollow as Georgie's chest when I reach into it and rip out his heart.

It looks so…mediocre. I can't believe the world revolves around this piece of meat that evokes things I don't understand like…love.

"And forgive us our trespasses as we forgive those who trespass against us; and lead us not into temptation, but deliver us from evil," I whisper, holding the heart to the light and closing one eye, desperate to see what the fuss is about.

I don't, however, and that's because I'm as dead as Georgie

is.

I peer down at my handiwork and smile. *"Daddy is proud of you, baby girl."*

I hear his voice just as I always do when I do something bad. I know this is my mind playing tricks on me, helping me cope with the atrocities I commit and do so with a smile.

I only hear his voice because I don't know what my mother sounds like. She ensured to take her secrets to the grave by cutting out her own tongue. She'd rather be a coward than own up to her sins and face her maker.

I know who she is and where she is, thanks to Gianna. I owe Gianna everything.

But when I hear another voice, the voice which has comforted and taunted me in the same breath, my bloody dream soon turns into a nightmare.

"Amen," he says, and I turn slowly to see him standing in the doorway, casually lighting a cigarette.

He wears black ripped jeans, boots, and a black shirt with three buttons undone, revealing that tattooed, muscled chest I know too well because I have laid my head against it, listening to *his* heart and believing in a thing called love…only for him to rip it away.

Our eyes lock, and I know what I've done because the man I just killed was his. *He* is Gianna's competition. *He* was also her faithful student once upon a time, only to turn against her and use her secrets to build his own empire.

Unlike *him*, I value loyalty.

I was to do this, knowing it would start a war.

But I didn't care because when I look into those blue-gray eyes, eyes I'd been lost in since I was a child, I knew this would bring *him* back to me. And there's a reason for it.

"You're in so much trouble, *tesoro mio*," he coolly says, blowing out the match.

He tongues his upper lip, and I remember what it felt like when I clung to that tall, muscled body and kissed the ever-living fuck out of that mouth. The mouth that kissed and defiled every inch of my body.

I also remember when that mouth uttered the lie, "*Ti amo.*"

Those memories have me climbing off the cooling corpse and tossing the heart of his man at his feet. "I wouldn't have it any other way."

It's been five years, but I can see that time hasn't healed all wounds. I wish time would have erased my feelings for him, but they haven't. All they've done is make me miss him all the more.

He smiles that slanted grin, and I die a thousand deaths because I lied…I do feel something.

I always have.

In the most dire circumstances, we found one another, and I thought he was my forever. But forever came with an expiration date when he became the enemy.

Lennon Shepherd…the man I love with every beat of my heart, is the man I must kill because if I don't…he'll kill me.

He'll kill me because I have been guarding a secret, a secret so grave, Lennon will never forgive me when he finds out the truth. But if I don't tell him, then someone else will.

Regardless of our feud, this is the one thing we will both fight for.

But when he enters the room and closes the door behind him, I know it isn't that simple. But nothing with Lennon ever is.

It's war…

CHAPTER 1

VALENTINA

TEN YEARS OLD

"You're stupid and ugly! Ugly! Ugly! Uglllllyyyyy!" chant a group of kids as I crouch into a small ball in the middle of the circle they form around me.

I don't know why they pick on me. I keep to myself and don't cause any trouble, but it doesn't make a difference. This happens every lunchtime behind the playground. And just like the many times before this, I don't fight back.

I want to.

But I don't, and that's because I'm an abomination in the

eyes of the Lord, and this is my punishment. That's what the sisters tell me anyway. They don't lie because they're the chosen ones. They are here to do God's work, and they've told me I need the most work here in the orphanage.

The other kids' souls are salvageable, but mine was tarnished from the day I was born. I must repent every single day for my sins in hopes that the Lord will show mercy on me. But it's hard to believe in His presence when someone throws a rock at my head.

I feel the familiar trickle of blood down my temple. I've lost count of how many cuts and bruises I have. I guess they all just form one big wound that never heals.

My brown hair is pulled. My cheek slapped. I don't know who does what because my eyes are squeezed shut. I hope that if I can't see what they're doing to me, then maybe it isn't happening. But when I'm kicked in the stomach, there's no escaping this reality of my life.

"Children, that is enough!"

The voice belongs to Father Merry.

I instantly wish I was knocked out cold because that punishment is far kinder than what is coming my way.

"What's going on here?"

I feel Father Merry's hands on me as he helps me stand. But I still don't open my eyes. I'm scared.

"She took the Lord's name in vain," says Hugo, a boy two

years older than me.

Hugo has hated me since the day he arrived at the orphanage. I don't know why he does. But they all do. And when I ask why, they say because my mother turned her back on God and fell in love with a bad man, and as a result, I was born.

They call me a monster.

Maybe I am? Why else would I be punished this way?

"Is that true, Valentina?"

I dare not open my eyes. I can't because the moment I see his face, I will remember all the things he's done.

I remain mute, which only irritates Father Merry.

"Come with me." I don't have a choice in the matter as he latches onto my arm and drags me from the playground.

I dig in my heels, which only infuriates him further. He picks me up and throws me over his shoulder.

My eyes are still closed, but I don't need to see where we're headed. I've been here before. I know it'll hurt. It always does. But my pain brings him pleasure. The more I resist, the harder he punishes me.

I push down my tears because they don't do me any good.

When the door opens and I smell frankincense, I instantly want to vomit. I associate the scent with the memory of when Father Merry first punished me. I was bent over a pew, where he used a large wooden crucifix to smack my bare bottom.

He smacked me so hard, I couldn't sit for a week. He left a

crucifix imprint behind to remind me that I am nothing but a sinner.

"You're just like your mother," he spits, closing the door to his office. "She is a coward like you. She left you on the doorstep, knowing you would bring her nothing but suffering. So you can thank your mother, Sister Margarette, for every lick of my belt."

He places me on my feet and slaps my cheek. "Open your eyes!"

I still don't.

I hear his belt being yanked through his pants loops before he roughly turns me and positions me over his desk. He yanks up the hem of my white dress and tears off my Minnie Mouse underwear. They were my favorite.

"Recite the Lord's Prayer," he orders like he does every time.

I bite my lip in defiance.

For my disobedience, he slaps me on the bottom with his belt.

"Our Father…" he begins, hoping to coax me.

But I remain silent.

Whack!

This strike is harder than the first, but I still don't budge.

"Who art in heaven…"

Smack!

I grip the edge of the desk, my tiny fingers holding on tightly as he continues hitting me while reciting a prayer that is supposed to denote love and devotion.

The entire time, I don't speak. I don't cry. I simply detach myself from my body and look down at the small, skinny girl who is being abused by someone who is supposed to protect her.

I hate my mother. She's the reason I'm here, and she's the reason the sisters and Father Merry despise me. They once were her family, a family she turned her back on when she had me.

I don't know where she is, but I need to find her. There has to be a reason she abandoned me when I was only hours old. What sins could I have committed so young for her to hate me that much?

What did I do to deserve this?

"Amen," Father Merry pants as he drops the belt to the floor.

But I know this isn't over. This is just the beginning.

He rubs over my raw bottom, tracing over the bloody welts with his finger. "For this is my blood of the covenant, which is poured out for many for forgiveness of sins."

I hold back my tears.

His zipper is lowered, the rubbing of skin makes me gag, and then—then I hear him hum a nursery rhyme which indicates what's ahead.

Ring around the rosie…

This is the moment I squeeze my eyes shut harder than before and force myself to disassociate with what is about to happen. Because the moment I feel the familiar burn between my legs, I know Father Merry is leaving a piece of himself inside me and robbing me of my soul.

I lay on my tattered blankets, peering out the barred window in my room in the attic. The mice that share my stale bread are my only friends. They keep me warm at night.

I don't share a bedroom with the other children. But I don't mind. I prefer to be alone.

My body aches all over. I'm caked in dry blood from what happened today in Father Merry's office.

"You are a vessel for God's spirit," he groaned before I felt something warm and sticky trickle down my thighs. "And I'm doing His work."

When he was done, he told me to leave. He wouldn't punish me further for my sins, sins I never committed because Hugo was lying, as long as I kept what we did private.

Tears I've kept away creep to the surface, and I begin to cry. I only allow myself this comfort when alone because crying is a sign of weakness. I learned that from my only friend in this place—Margot Henson. She was the only person who showed me any kindness.

She was four years older than me, and she too was Father

Merry's favorite. One evening, we were dragged from our beds and brought to the basement where four men waited for us. Father Merry was one of them. They smelled of cigars and wine.

We took turns being their favorites all night, but when Margot began to cry, it seemed that she was then the favored one. I tried to help her when two men took turns making her cry the loudest. When she did, they silenced her cries with their fingers or…other things.

When Father Merry finished with me, I jumped up and kicked one of the men in the shin. It was hopeless, however, because I was knocked out cold for my rebellion. When I came to, I was back in my bed, but Margot was not.

For weeks, I didn't see her, but when I finally did and saw the swelling in her belly, I realized no matter how many tears are shed, cruelty will always prevail.

I haven't shed a single tear in company since.

The moon is full, allowing the shadows to dance across the lawn. This place is like a castle the wicked witch in any Disney movie would live in. But it's the only home I know.

I've not been allowed to watch TV in a little while, but when I did, I was fascinated by the movies with families laughing and smiling, where things were always light and never black, which is what my world is. I live in the shadows because I want to blend into the darkness.

I want to disappear.

Does that world really exist? If He is good, why does nothing but bad happen to me?

Something shiny catches my eye from outside, interrupting my thoughts.

Quickly sitting up, I wipe away my tears so I can get a better look at who is in the gardens in the middle of the night.

It's a boy I've not seen before.

He looks tall, and his hair is brown. But apart from that, I can't make out much else.

I watch in interest as he crouches low and slowly begins moving toward a large hedge. I don't know why, but his movements leave me breathless. I feel like I'm watching a predator stalk his prey.

It seems impossible, but the closer he gets, the darkness seems to wrap him further into the shadows, where I almost can't see him. I want to be like that because he isn't afraid of the dark; it bends to his will. Even nature seems to be under his spell.

He stops as if measuring the right moment, and when he lunges forward and produces a tiny ball of white fluff in his hand, I realize that he truly is a hunter.

The white fluffball is a kitten. It's tiny, and I wonder where its mother is. Was it also abandoned?

I get onto my knees and interlock my fingers through the bars, needing to get a closer view of the mystery boy. He pats the kitten before slipping him into the pocket of his sweater. I don't know why, but the gesture touches me.

To be cared for that way must be nice.

He peers from left to right before walking back toward the orphanage. He isn't in any hurry, not bothered that he is outside unsupervised. I wonder how he got out. I also wonder why he isn't running away. But where would he go? Where would any of us go?

We don't have any family, which is why we're here.

He is almost out of sight but suddenly stops. A breath catches in my throat when he lifts his chin slowly, and our eyes lock. Even from this distance away, I know he can see me. He caught me spying.

I quickly retreat, embarrassed I've been caught.

But then I do something bold. I slowly reemerge, only to see him standing in the same spot, peering up at the window.

Under the starless sky, we simply stare at one another.

His long hair falls over one eye, but there is no question that he is striking. He is also brave.

He lifts a hand, and it's a gesture that I reciprocate because no one has waved at me before. No one has cared enough about me to say hello.

And then he disappears into the shadows like he never really existed at all.

The only proof that he was real is the thumping of my heart.

CHAPTER 2

VALENTINA

I'm allowed to eat breakfast in the dining hall with everyone else today, and I know that means we'll be lined up and paraded around in hopes of being adopted.

It's always the same; optimistic parents enter through the doors in hopes of finding their perfect child. It goes without saying that I am no one's first, second, or even last choice. I'm overlooked because I'm too much work.

No one wants to adopt a scrawny child with eyes too big for her freckled face. The other children wear their best clothes and comb their hair, while I'm in dresses two sizes too big and shoes with worn-down soles.

The bruises and cuts I constantly sport make me look like a troublemaker. If only they knew how I obtained them. But no one seems to care. The sisters stopped listening a long time ago as they knew my mother and didn't want anything to do with me, afraid my wickedness would rub off on them somehow.

I am alone.

I'm eating my watery porridge, keeping my head down. But it doesn't matter. It seems trouble always follows me.

"Who let you out of your cage?" Hugo laughs as he sits across from me.

I clench the spoon in my hand but don't react.

"Deaf and stupid. No wonder your mom abandoned you. I heard she's had ten children. They all live happily with her in a mansion by the beach. You're the only one she didn't want because you're a reject."

The spoon rattles against the bowl as I try to contain my temper.

"Are you going to cry?" he mocks, and when I continue to ignore him, he flips my bowl, spilling porridge all down the front of my dress.

The room erupts into laughter.

My cheeks heat under my long hair, which shields my face. I wish I was brave like the boy I saw last night. He wouldn't sit here with spilled breakfast down his clothes. He would fight back.

So for the first time in my life, I slowly lift my chin and lock eyes with Hugo.

He gasps, as I think it's the first time he's ever seen my blue eyes, eyes which Father Merry calls eyes of the devil as they're identical to my mother's. And right now, I use that wickedness to ram the spoon I'm holding into Hugo's eye.

I don't even think twice about the repercussions. It comes naturally. I like it.

He does not like it, as I can imagine a spoon being impaled into one's eyeball would be quite painful. He grows silent before the reality of what I've done sinks in, and a pained howl echoes off the walls.

He leaps from the seat, the spoon embedded into his eyeball.

I can't help but laugh.

"Daddy's girl," a voice randomly says in my head. It scares me because I've not heard it before. But it sounds familiar. I just don't know why.

He tries to pull it out but screams in pain and, instead, blindly flails around the room. The kids shrink away as he begs for help. They don't want to get involved. I simply sit back and smile at the chaos I've created.

Suddenly, the same feelings as last night overwhelm me. I look across the table and see the boy who's never left my mind since I first saw him. He coolly takes the same seat Hugo was sitting in before he had a spoon wedged into his eyeball.

He doesn't say a word.

And neither do I.

We're both calm in the chaos.

I examine him closely because I feel a connection to him that I can't explain. His eyes are the strangest color—a mixture of blue and gray, reminding me of the bluest skies before the storm clouds roll in, the chaos replacing the calm. His brown hair is longer on top with shorter sides. He's older than me. I would guess eleven or twelve. But he seems more mature than his years.

I wonder how long he's been here.

He's wearing a black T-shirt with holes that it seems he ripped in the material. I see he has a gold necklace around his neck. The pendant is round and looks to be a compass. I wonder what it means. He has on torn black jeans and scuffed boots with the laces untied.

He smiles, and I like it. So I smile back. It feels strange. I'm not used to smiling. So I hope I don't scare him away.

He leans across the table and steals someone's porridge mid-bite. They dare not object because they don't fancy joining Hugo.

"Eat," he orders, sliding the bowl toward me. Who knew that word would be the first one spoken.

He offers me a spoon, and when the doors burst open, and three sisters come running into the room to see what the noise is about, he nods in a gesture that I can trust him.

I don't know why, but I do.

I accept the spoon, but when he stands, I don't understand why. That is, until he walks over to Hugo and punches him in the ribs.

My hands fly up to my mouth. What is he doing?

The sisters scream for help, but the boy raises his hands in surrender.

Father Merry comes charging into the room, and when he sees the boy, he shakes his head in anger. "You're nothing but trouble, Lennon!"

And the boy has a name—Lennon.

"You've been here for less than a month, and you're getting into fights already. You're going to be punished for this! You're going to see Saint Maria's doesn't tolerate hoodlums, and you're nothing but a little punk!"

He grabs him by the arm and drags him from the room. But I can't stand by and let him take the blame for something he didn't do.

I jump up, ready to tell Father Merry I was the one who hurt Hugo, but Lennon places a finger over his lips. Why is he taking the blame? I don't understand.

"It was—" I don't get a chance to finish because Lennon

turns around and headbutts Father Merry in the nose. Blood instantly pours down his face.

It's utter bedlam, and when Lennon is dragged from the room with a grin on his face, I know he just saved me.

But why?

I'm mopping the long hallway as Sister Siobhan ordered when she saw the state I was in. "No one will want to adopt you," she said in disgust. "You look a fright. For penance, you can mop the halls because cleanliness is next to godliness."

And it's here I've been all day, mopping while the other kids have a chance at a new life.

My hands are sore because of the blisters on them. But I persevere because I'm hoping I'll cross paths with Lennon. I need to ask him why he took the blame for me. I knew the consequences that came with my actions, but he didn't think twice as he saved me from being punished for my sins.

Father Merry suddenly appears, and I lower my face, my bravado gone into hiding. "You've done a good job," he says, reaching out and lifting my chin so he can look into my eyes.

Is he searching for the truth?

"For your efforts, you'll be rewarded."

I gulp as there is no such thing when Father Merry is

involved.

"I will come get you this evening. I'm expecting guests. You'd like that, wouldn't you?"

I don't say a word.

"You're as stubborn as your mother was. But look where that got her. Don't make the same mistakes she did."

He grips my chin so hard, my lips purse, and when he licks his, I want to punch him in the face. I know what he's thinking, and although I've not been taught about such matters, I know this is wrong.

When Father Merry hears footsteps approaching, he quickly releases me. "Did you give penance, Lennon?"

I suddenly feel braver with Lennon close by.

"I'm all penanced out," he replies, not bothering to mask his sarcasm.

Father Merry's lips pull into a thin line, but he doesn't respond.

He cups my cheek, nodding in a promise that he will see me tonight, then he leaves.

I grip the wooden handle of the mop, my body trembling in anger. I want to choke him with my bare hands. The cross above the hallway mocks me because there is no God. Or if there is, he doesn't believe in me.

"Why did you do that?" I ask, my back turned to Lennon.

"Because they both deserved it."

"No," I say, turning around to face him. But what I see has me gasping. "Wh-what happened to your face?"

"I slipped," he counters with a cocky grin.

But I know he too is the victim of Father Merry's cruelty.

He has a blackening eye, and his lip is split open.

"Why did you take the blame?" I whisper, chewing my bottom lip.

He reaches out and gently releases my lip with his thumb. "Because it was the right thing to do."

I blink once, unsure what that means.

"What's your name?"

"My name?" I ask, confused.

"You have a name, don't you?"

I nod, but I explain my cause for concern. "No one has asked me before."

"Well, their loss," Lennon says, folding his arms across his chest. "So what's your name?"

"It's Valentina," I reply, my voice small.

He mulls over my strange name but smiles.

"What's your name?"

"Lennon Shepherd, but you can call me Lenny. What happened?" he asks, gesturing with his chin toward my many cuts and bruises.

Instantly, I feel my cheeks redden because, to someone like Lenny, I'm nothing but a weak coward.

"What you did today took guts," he says as if reading my thoughts. "Don't ever forget it."

I want to ask him so many questions, but I've not spoken to anyone in a long time. I've almost forgotten what it feels like.

He reaches for the mop and wrings it in the bucket before he starts mopping the hall.

"What are you doing?"

"Mopping the floor," he replies with a mischievous grin.

"But why?"

"Do you always ask so many questions?"

I can't help but smile. It feels foreign.

"I saw you last night."

"I saw you too."

"Where's the kitten?"

He looks up and down the hallway, ensuring we're alone. "He's in a safe place. Want to see?"

I nod happily.

"Okay, I'll come get you tonight."

My stomach drops as I remember Father Merry's words. "I can't tonight."

I'm afraid if Father Merry finds us together, the same fate will befall Lenny. And I don't want that for him. I want to save him just as he saved me.

He pauses from mopping and tilts his head to the side, examining me closely.

I shuffle my feet nervously.

"Why not?"

"Do you always ask so many questions?" I counter, using his words back at him.

He laughs. "Touché. You've got guts. Use it on whoever gave you this." He reaches out and brushes back a piece of hair, touching the wound at my temple.

His touch is foreign as it's filled with kindness. It's the first time I've experienced such compassion.

"I'm not brave."

He gently cups my cheek, those beautiful eyes penetrating right through me. "You can be whatever you want to be. You just have to believe it."

A tear slides down my cheek, but I quickly wipe it away, embarrassed. "Where are your parents?"

"Dead," he replies calmly.

"Oh, I'm sorry."

"Don't be. They deserved it. I've bounced from foster home to foster home, but once they got sick of me escaping, they sent me here—to hell. I need to get out of here. I need to find my brother. They separated us, which is why I kept escaping."

"You were trying to find him?"

He nods, his jaw clenched.

I don't know what it is about Lenny, but he touches something inside me. He makes me feel…worthy.

"I want to help."

"See, there she is, my brave Valentina. You don't even know me, and you want to help. I could be a serial killer for all you know."

"No, that was my dad," I reveal, and when Lenny sees I'm serious, his mouth drops open. "His name was Patrick O'Loughlin."

"Damn," Lenny says, shaking his head in awe. "And I thought my dad was an asshole."

I don't know what to say, so I do what feels natural—I laugh.

Lenny looks at me before he too joins in with the laughter. "You're not like anyone I've ever met before."

"Neither are you," I reply, smiling broadly—another first.

He seems to grow quiet when our laughter dies, as if listening for something I don't hear. "I'll finish up here."

I don't want to go and wonder if maybe I said something wrong. But when I hear the voices of approaching sisters, I realize he doesn't want me to be roped into doing any more chores for the day.

He rests the mop handle in the crook of his armpit so he can reach for both of my calloused hands. He turns them over, and a look of anger slashes across his face. "Go."

It's not a suggestion but rather an order.

I leave him watching me protectively, and only when I am out of sight do I hear the mop swish against the linoleum.

The moment the pull-down steps whine, hinting someone is coming up, I roll onto my side. I hope if I fake sleep, Father Merry will go away.

His footsteps creak across the wooden flooring, each step sending my heart into overdrive. I can smell the liquor on his breath as he leans down and kisses the top of my head.

"You look just like her. My sweet Margarette."

I can't breathe when he runs his hand down my back.

"You've got guts. Use it on whoever gave you this."

Lenny's words echo in my head, but I don't know how to fight Father Merry off. He will; he *has* overpowered me. And I am so tired of fighting a battle I can never win.

"Come now, sweetling, my friends are waiting. Let's get you cleaned up first."

I'm lax in his arms as he carries me from the attic to the bathroom, where he bathes me. This is the only time he's gentle.

"Water and baptism symbolize the Lord's death, burial, and resurrection. It is in water we purify ourselves of our sins and become one with the Lord," he says, passing the soapy cloth over my body.

His touches never stray from that of a caregiver when he prepares me like this. I wonder if he thinks he's doing the right thing to make amends for all the awful things he's about to commit.

Once I'm clean, he dresses me in a long white nightgown. He then plaits my hair into two braids.

He takes my hand, and we commence our familiar walk down the deserted hallway. I'm not nervous. I know what to expect, and the moment the basement door comes into view, I detach from my mind so I can no longer feel the atrocities that are about to befall me.

Father Merry opens the door, and we descend the stairs. I can smell cigarette smoke. I can hear the familiar whimpers.

Our hands are still entwined when we enter the basement.

"Gentlemen, forgive me for taking so long," he says, addressing the two men who sit around a poker table.

Another man is behind the white sheet that's hung up to provide privacy. I can see his silhouette. It's lit up by the dim lighting. The lighting also allows me to see someone on their knees, their head bobbing up and down.

Still, I feel nothing. I have switched off to this reality because I want to believe it's a nightmare I'll wake from one day soon.

"She is worth the wait, Father. Bring her to me. I need a closer look."

Father Merry leads me over to the man. I know better than to meet the eyes of these men, so I keep my head bowed. I can see he has shiny black shoes and wears navy trousers. He isn't a man of God. Could he be different from the others?

"My name is Aldo," he calmly says in an accent I've never heard.

No one has ever told me their name before.

"What's your name?"

I don't respond because I know I can't speak to these men.

"It's okay, *bellezza*. Don't be afraid."

"Her name is—" Father Merry commences but is sharply cut off by Aldo.

"I didn't ask you, Father. I asked her."

No one has ever spoken to Father Merry this way.

I like it.

I find the courage to speak. "Valentina," I say, wetting my dry lips.

"Valentina. A beautiful name for a beautiful little girl. Look at me, Valentina."

Even though this is against all the "rules," I slowly lift my chin and look at Aldo.

He has dark hair and green eyes. They aren't bloodshot or unfocused like the other men who have sat where he is. He seems gracious.

"That's better. Look at those blue eyes. Eyes of an angel."

Father Merry shifts uncomfortably, and I like that he seems uneasy.

"Come, we're going to have a talk."

He stands and offers me his hand.

Father Merry still has my hand but lets it go when Aldo makes clear this isn't negotiable.

I slowly walk over to Aldo, who is much taller up close. He also smells nice. He smiles down at me. I simply stare at him, confused.

"Come, Valentina." I cautiously slip my hand into his and follow as he leads me around the corner.

Old Christmas decorations and broken furniture are strewn around. It's dark and dank, but funnily enough, I'm not afraid.

"I am very sorry you have lived this life, *bellezza*."

I don't know what that word means, but it's kind.

"But I wish to take you away from here. Would you like that?"

I don't know what to say. Is this a trick?

When Aldo sees my apprehension, he smiles. "It's all right. I will not hurt you. You are far too precious for that. The paperwork is being finalized, but you will come live with me very soon."

So many thoughts race around my head. No one has ever wanted me before. I don't understand why Aldo does.

"I need two of you, though. A boy. Is there someone you'd like to take with you?"

I nod quickly in case he changes his mind.

"What is his name?"

I clear my throat, desperate to find my voice. "L-Lennon."

"Okay, I will make sure of it."

I don't know what to say because this is surely a dream.

"I promise this life will be no more, *bellezza*. I hope everything will be organized in days. Until then, I will try to keep you safe."

"Why me?" I whisper, confused. "I am nothing. No one."

But Aldo clucks his tongue as he brushes his thumb along the apple of my cheek. "Don't let me hear you say that ever again. You are far braver than you know. You must believe in yourself because you are going to change the world."

I don't know how, but I want to believe Aldo.

"No one has ever been this kind to me," I confess, still unbelieving this is true. "What do you want from me?"

A hoarse laugh leaves Aldo. "I want that." When I arch a brow in confusion, he clarifies. "I want that fighting spirit. I need it to succeed. You are invaluable to me."

Father Merry sheepishly appears. "Everything all right? She isn't what you wanted?"

I curl my lip, disgusted to be spoken about in this way.

Aldo grins, pleased his words aren't lost on me. "She is exactly what I want. She is to go to her room. No other man will touch her. I will come get her once the paperwork is signed."

There is no negotiation. Aldo has laid down the rule.

"We did not discuss that," Father Merry says, shaking his

head. "She isn't up for adoption."

I narrow my eyes because this is the first time I've heard this. Is that why I've been stuck here? Because Father Merry has told potential parents just that?

I hate him all the more.

Anger bubbles to the surface, and I take a step forward, ready to punch Father Merry in the stomach, but Aldo gently places his large hand on my shoulder, stopping me.

"I will pay you a quarter of a million dollars for her."

Father Merry's mouth gapes wide because money talks. But I can see there is apprehension. And so can Aldo.

"Half a million then for two children. Valentina and Lennon. Both shall be in my care."

I don't know what to say because no one, *no one*, has ever wanted me.

"You can have Lennon, but not Valentina," Father Merry firmly says, folding his arms.

Visions of ramming a jagged edge of the broken Christmas tree ornament into Father Merry's throat overwhelm me.

"*Bellezza*," Aldo warns as if reading my thoughts.

His voice calms me, and I back down—for now.

"Father, do you enjoy your life?"

Father Merry looks at Aldo, confused. "Not that it is any business of yours, but I do. I live to serve the Lord."

Aldo scoffs lightly. "Is that what you tell yourself when on your knees, praying to your God? Does that absolve you of your sins?"

"We are all God's children, and He loves us infinitely, regardless of the sins we commit. If we repent—"

"Save your sermons, Father. They are wasted on a man like me," Aldo orders calmly. "In three days, I will come for Valentina and Lennon. I will give you your money, and then we will never see one another ever again."

"I beg your—" But Father Merry never finishes his sentence because Aldo coolly reaches into the back of his pants and produces a gun. He aims it at Father Merry's head.

"Three days, Father," Aldo repeats, never wavering, while Father Merry looks seconds away from passing out. It's a sight I'll never forget.

Eventually, Father Merry concedes. "Why do you want her?"

Aldo grins, but it's not a happy gesture. "The same reason you do."

I spin around, wanting to ask what that reason is, but Aldo bops the end of my nose. "See you soon, *bellezza*. Stay out of trouble until then."

And that's it.

I am dismissed.

I have so many questions, but this is my way out, and I have to pick my battles to win the war. So I look at my savior one final time, hoping he'll be taking me away from this place.

I walk past Father Merry, but he doesn't move, and that's because Aldo's gun is still pointed at his head. I'm about to turn the corner when I hear a girl's muffled cry, which is soon drowned out by the squeaks of a mattress.

Squeak…

Squeak, squeak…

Squeak, squeak, squeak…

I know the sound all too well.

I want to help her, but Aldo shakes his head. "We can't save them all," he wisely says, knowing another would just take her place.

But how can I turn my back on her? I am here. I may not be able to save them all, but I can her. But in this circumstance, it's either me or her.

And I choose me, even if it's a choice I will regret for the rest of my life.

I hurry from the basement, my tiny legs barely able to keep up as I run to my room, afraid this is all a joke. But when I jump into my bed, heart racing so loudly I can hear it in my ears, I see that no one is following me.

I hold my breath, certain Father Merry will appear, telling me it's all a joke.

But he doesn't.

And only then do I take what feels like my first breath of life.

CHAPTER 3

VALENTINA

I'm on my hands and knees scrubbing the toilets, but I don't mind because I'll be gone tomorrow.

Aldo said three days.

Three days isn't a long time, but for me, each hour, each minute, has felt like ten thousand years. But I know my time has finally come.

So I persevere because I have hope.

The sisters have ensured my last days here are far from easy. But I'll happily scrub every toilet in this place because I know it's soon to be my last. I'm humming softly as I clean the boys' bathroom. The place is always a disgusting mess, so I'll be here for a while.

As I'm using the brush to clean around the toilet bowl, I hear the door open.

"Occupied!" I call out, not bothering to stop scrubbing. "Use the bathroom down the hall."

Rushed footsteps echo from behind, but I don't have time to turn around before someone grips my hair and slams my face into the ceramic bowl. I use my hands to stop from connecting with the toilet a second time, but my attacker pulls my head back hard, allowing me to see him.

"Nice eye patch," I mock, trying to remain composed because Hugo, my attacker, is intent on revenge.

"I lost my eye because of you!" he snarls, inches from my face.

"Too bad I didn't cut out your tongue."

Hugo snarls and attempts to drag me out of the stall. But I grip the bowl using my arms and legs. If I don't fight, I'm scared I will be leaving the orphanage in a body bag.

Revenge makes Hugo strong and brave. He punches me in the temple, and my vision instantly blurs.

My grip slackens, and Hugo drags me along the floor by my hair. I try to grab onto something, but the floor is slippery thanks to it being recently mopped. I kick my legs out and attempt to pry myself free from Hugo's grip, but he only pulls my hair harder.

"Help!" I scream, hating that I can't defend myself.

But Hugo silences me when he reaches for the mop and shoves it into my mouth.

Instantly, I taste detergent and dry retch because that is beyond disgusting. I cleaned the entire bathroom with this mop. I know what revolting things I mopped up. He removes it, only to snap the handle in half as he brings it over his knee.

I wonder what he intends to do with it.

Things happen so fast, and Hugo has the advantage because he knows what he wants. He is the predator. I am his prey.

When he lets go of my hair, I scramble frantically, but Hugo jumps on top of me, pinning me to the floor. I reach out with my free hand and slap his cheek.

This only enrages him further.

He punches me in the face, resulting in the back of my head slamming against the hard floor. My nose begins to bleed. I'm not sure if it's broken. I can't feel pain anymore.

Hugo won't be happy until I'm dead. But when he yanks up the hem of my dress, it's apparent he would prefer another outcome over my death.

Fight or flight takes over, and ignoring my injuries, I begin to fight with every ounce of strength I have. I kick my legs. I rear up and bite Hugo's neck. But it's all in vain when I feel his fingers penetrate me crudely.

He doesn't care that it hurts so badly I can taste blood from biting down on my tongue. He just continues to violently assault me, keeping me pinned down with his forearm over my throat, watching me with his one eye.

He's getting off on this. He's just as sick as all the other men who have violated me. Every part of my body hurts. As does my soul. How many times can this happen to me before I drift away and am never found?

I detach from my body, just as I always do, but Hugo won't allow it.

"No, bitch, look at me!" He spits in my face and slaps my cheek. "You're wet. You like it. You're nothing but a filthy whore. I would fuck you, but my cock is too good for your diseased cunt. But you need to be taught a lesson."

He reaches for the broken mop handle, and my question as to why he snapped it in half is answered as he removes his fingers from me, intending to replace them with something else.

"No!" I wheeze, flailing with the last shred of fight I have left.

But it's fruitless when I feel the most grotesque pain splitting my body into two, followed by Hugo's elated, victorious screams.

I stop fighting because I am robbed of life.

Robbed of breath.

I can't feel any part of my body any longer. It stops hurting, but I know that's not because Hugo has stopped raping me with a household item that is supposed to represent cleanliness.

I will never be clean ever again.

Hugo bites my neck, whispering into my ear what a good girl I am as he continues violating me with that handle, and just as I close my eyes, surrendering to defeat, fate reveals it's not done with me just yet.

The only reason I know this is really happening is Hugo's pained screams for help are a salve to my blistering soul. I realize the pain between my legs is an echo because I'm no longer being assaulted. But my attacker didn't stop of his own accord.

He stopped because someone was delivering to him what he did to me.

All I can hear is fists connecting with bone and flesh, but instead of recoiling, I rejoice because it's music to my soul.

Opening my eyes, I slowly lift myself onto one elbow and focus on the scene before me.

Who I see has me realizing I made the right choice when Aldo asked who I wanted to come with me.

Lenny punches and kicks Hugo on the floor while he's curled into a ball, begging him to stop. But Lenny doesn't stop. In fact, he only seems to grow more incensed as he continues to beat the living hell out of Hugo.

"I'm sorry!"

Punch.

"I didn't mean—"

Kick.

However, Lenny isn't listening, and when Hugo begins crying, he kicks him in the ribs until he collapses onto his stomach. What he does next, I take complete delight in because an eye for an eye…figuratively speaking, of course.

He yanks down Hugo's trousers and reaches for the handle that was used on me in the most brutal of ways.

He doesn't speak.

He doesn't hesitate.

He drives the handle into Hugo's ass and inflicts the same treatment on him as he did to me.

Hugo's pained screams excite me, and the deeper Lenny shoves that handle into Hugo's ass, the nervous energy inside me explodes, and I am breathless with exhilaration. Something must be very wrong with me because this doesn't disgust me. On the contrary, I want to see Hugo's blood.

Pushing past my pain, I come to a shaky stand, and when Lenny meets my eyes, he nods.

"Finish it," he orders, knowing this is my fight.

Hugo has passed out from shock, but that won't do.

I look down at the pathetic boy who has been reduced to nothing but a crybaby and wonder what I ever did for him to hate me so much. But at this moment, I realize that sometimes there isn't a reason.

Bad things happen because there are bad people in this world, and…I think I'm one of them.

Hugo's tears stain his cheeks, but I don't feel a slither of remorse for what I'm about to do. I yank out the mop handle, which has Hugo coming back to life as his entire body jolts. I toss it away and kick him onto his back.

He winces as I straddle him.

He doesn't fight. He simply looks at me, begging I show mercy.

"You picked on the wrong girl," I state calmly because, for the first time ever, I'm the one in control. "Let this be a lesson learned."

Reaching for the container of bleach, I unscrew the cap, and when Hugo clamps his lips shut, I pull up his eye patch and drive my thumb into his empty eye socket.

His screams are pained.

My laughs are elated.

I pour the bleach down Hugo's throat and cackle maniacally when he begins to gag on the poisonous fluid.

"And that lesson is…be nice."

I hold his mouth closed by placing my hand over it, forcing him to swallow as I pinch his nose and slap his cheek. When he does, I release him and come to a stand. "Good boy."

I watch as he clutches his throat, convulsing on the floor as foam spills from his mouth.

Lennon stands by me, arms folded as he too watches Hugo squirming on the floor.

We're both unmoved.

Turning to look at Lenny, I see he has flecks of Hugo's blood on his face, and on instinct, I stand on tippy-toes and run my thumb along the blood trail, smudging it so it stains down his eye and onto his cheek. A single red line mars his face, and he's never looked more heroic and beautiful than he does right now.

Warpaint on a warrior who saved my life.

"Let's go." He links our fingers and leads us from the bathroom.

The hallway is quiet because everyone is in Mass. We quickly walk to the attic. Once we climb the stairs, I realize Lennon is the first guest I've had up here. When he sees the state of my "room," my cheeks blush. I'm embarrassed he has seen where I live.

I attempt to tidy things up, but he grips my forearm, stopping me. "Are you all right?"

No one has ever asked me that before. I'm not okay. I haven't been for my entire life. But I nod.

"You probably need to see the nurse."

"I'm fine." Pain radiates in my belly and backside, but I quash it down because there is no way I'm going to the infirmary. "We're getting out of here. Tomorrow."

"We are?"

"Yes."

"How do you know that?"

How can I disclose what I know without divulging to Lennon what happened? I don't want him looking at me differently. I don't want him to know what Father Merry has done to me over the years. What if he sees me as weak?

What if he sees me as a victim?

"I just do." I settle for that reply, making it clear I don't want to talk about it.

He doesn't press, but I can see by the tight purse of his lips that he finds it hard to believe. I don't blame him. It feels as if we're never going to leave this place. And we're doomed to remain here until the end of time.

Lenny looks at me, and I suddenly realize what a mess I must look. I wipe my bloody nose with the back of my hand. But it just smudges across my face.

"Here."

Before I can object, Lennon removes his T-shirt and wipes my face. I shrink away, not wanting to be tended to this way, but he grips my upper arm to stop me from moving. My scrawny arm doesn't stand a chance against his big hands.

I allow him to tend to me, and although I'm not accustomed to such kindness, I don't mind it coming from Lennon. He isn't gentle, but I can feel the tenderness behind his touch. I don't understand why he's come into my life or why I feel this pull toward him, but I'm glad he is here.

"What secrets are you hiding, little girl?"

"Why do you think I'm hiding anything? And I'm not a little girl." I pull out of his grip, not wishing to be treated like a baby.

He has the audacity to laugh. "Yes, you are. But you're far braver than a hundred men, which is why I think your secrets made you this courageous. You were forced to be brave. It's either kill or be killed. But here you are. I want to know everything about you."

I hold my breath.

No one has ever shown interest in me before. I'm used to blending into the background and not existing. But Lenny is different. I want him to know about me because I want to know about him.

He does something that forever ties us—he wipes the blood from my wounds with two fingers and smudges them across his lips, leaving behind a smear of red. Before I can ask what he's doing, he then runs his fingers along his bloody knuckles and glides them across my mouth so I'm coated in his blood.

"This is my body. This is my blood," he says, reciting something I've heard in Mass many times. But spoken from Lenny's bloody lips, it takes on a whole different meaning.

Our blood has forever linked us and sealed our destiny in

a bloodstained kiss.

I suddenly feel tired, and I realize it's because I feel safe. I know Lenny won't hurt me. A yawn slips past my lips.

"Go to sleep. I'll be here when you wake up."

I want to argue, but my eyelids grow heavy of their own accord. I force them open, but Lenny gently cups my cheek.

"Sleep."

It's evident Lenny doesn't take no for an answer, so I do as he says. I lay on my dirty mattress and turn on my side to look at him. He stands watch between me and the door. And he doesn't waver from his post just as he promised he wouldn't.

This is the first night I sleep and don't dream.

CHAPTER 4

LENNY

She sleeps like the dead. And perhaps she wishes she was. I don't know what she's endured, but I know it's bad. I know she's broken, and I don't think she'll ever heal. But she isn't a victim. She has fire behind her eyes, and one day, I have no doubt that fire will burn this kingdom to the ground.

And I can't wait to be by her side when she does.

I don't understand why I feel this urgent need to protect her. It was there from the moment I saw her. Perhaps it's because I see myself in her in the sense we are both broken, lost, and alone. But we don't allow that to define us because we fight.

We fight because there must be more to life than…this.

Valentina…such a strange name for an extraordinary girl.

She said we're getting out of here. But how?

Regardless, I believe her.

The latch door opens, and without thought, I turn my back toward Valentina, standing between her and whoever creeps into her room in the early hours of the morning before the sun has even risen. She's been out cold for hours, but the moment the hinges on the door whine, the sound startles her awake.

I look over my shoulder and see her spring up and scamper across the mattress and into the corner of the room with her back pressed to the wall. Her eyes are wide. Her mouth agape as she gasps for air. She hides behind her long brown hair.

What the fuck happened to her?

When Father Merry appears at the top of the ladder, Valentina's whimpers hint that *he* is what happened to her.

I'm going to rip off his arms and beat him to death with them.

I give him a fright as he clearly was expecting her to be alone, but I stand my ground, arms folded, daring him to do his best because he won't hurt Valentina ever again. He composes himself as he lifts himself into the room.

"It is forbidden for you to be in here," he scolds, his beady little eyes narrowing.

"Same goes for you, asshole. The church is thataway." I hook my thumb over my shoulder. "Did you get lost?"

"I don't suppose you know anything about Hugo being attacked?"

"Nope," I reply, my gaze never wavering. "When you find out who did it, let me know so I can give them a high five."

"You are nothing but a sinner!" he bellows, charging forward.

I don't move, however, and when he comes to a stop inches away, I hear Valentina whimper.

He peers over my shoulder at her, which pisses me off.

"Hey, don't look at her," I warn, standing tall because I'm bigger than him. "Look at me."

"You're both sinners," he sneers, eyes still locked on her. "I should punish you both."

"For what?" I challenge. When he continues eyeballing her, I shift, shielding her with my form.

"I can guess what you were doing up here. You're nothing but a temptress, young lady," he says, and I suddenly know why Valentina is so scared of him.

And that's the reason I don't even think twice before I headbutt Father Merry in the face.

His nose squelches as he drops to the floor, howling in pain.

I grip him by the shirt and get into his face. "Listen here, you disgusting fuck, you will never talk, you will never look at her ever again. Got it?"

Father Merry simply snickers. "Who do you think you are? I will have you both thrown into solitary so you can repent for your sins."

It seems Father Merry isn't listening. So I headbutt him once again. The force snaps his neck backward since I'm still holding his shirt.

His head lolls to the side as I drag him inches away from my face. "I said, got...it?"

Bloody foam bubbles gather at the creases of his mouth as he tries to speak. But I grip his chin and force his head up and down.

"Good dog," I taunt, shoving him backward.

He falls onto his back, eyeing me something wicked. However, he knows better than to get up. He stays down, but I know this is the beginning of the end. If we don't get out of here like Valentina said, then we're about to suffer in ways unimaginable.

The gentle patter of feet across the cold floor calms me somewhat. Valentina is the only person who has that effect on me. She stands by me, peering down at Father Merry. I wonder what she sees.

She slowly turns to look at me and does something that surprised yet excited me when we were in the bathroom. Reaching up, she runs her thumb from the top of my eyebrow, over my eye, which I close, and down my cheek.

She pulls her thumb away, colored red from Father Merry's blood.

"I like this face best," she says in a dreamy voice.

"I do too. This face will always be yours," I reveal, wanting her to know that I'll always protect her no matter what happens.

She smiles, but that soon becomes a scowl when she gazes at Father Merry.

"One day, I'll come back for you. I don't know when. But I promise you will pay for everything you've done."

Father Merry backs away on his elbows as she casually walks toward him. He doesn't have a chance to flee before she kicks him in the ribs, winding him. She kicks him again and again, not holding back.

I see something change in her.

The shy, meek mouse is no more.

Valentina has found the killer within. Perhaps, that's the reason we have bonded this way—because we are one and the same.

We both feel alive in the bloodshed.

The final kick to Father Merry's face renders him unconscious.

She peers down at him, her pouty lip upturned. "Amen."

She spits on him before turning to me, her eyes alight. She knows that we cannot kill him up here. Too many questions will be asked.

I doubt Father Merry will tell anyone what happened because Valentina has someone on her side for once—she has me. And Father Merry knows that I will ensure everyone knows what a sick bastard he really is.

So he will lick his wounds in private.

Valentina takes one final look at the place she called home before descending the stairs. I follow, and when we're in the hallway, I take her hand and lead her to my room.

It's so quiet. Everyone is still asleep. It's my favorite time. I don't do people, so it's in the silence in which I feel most at ease. Valentina's hand is still in mine, and when I enter my dormitory, I head straight for my single bed.

The boys are sleeping soundly. Must be nice. I don't know what it's like to sleep without waking in a cold sweat, thanks to the soundtrack stuck on repeat of the screams of your parent burning alive waking you every goddamn night.

But I shake the memory from my mind because I have other pressing matters to deal with. The only source of light I have is the morning sun rising from behind the clouds, but it's enough. I reach into the pillowcase and am relieved that he's still here.

"Valentina, meet Cat. Cat, meet Valentina." I offer the white kitten to Valentina, but she suddenly looks afraid. "What's the matter?"

"I-I don't know how to hold him. What if I hurt him?"

"You won't."

Before she can question herself further, I gently place the kitten into her hands and coax her to hold him. A gasp leaves her as she peers up at me with those piercing blue eyes.

"He's so soft."

From her reaction, I guess she's never pet a cat before. I'm glad I was able to change that.

She strokes his fur, holding him close to her chest in a tight embrace. "I'm glad I saw you," she confesses guiltily.

"I am too."

She intrigued me from the moment I saw her because I wondered who the girl was, locked away in the attic like a princess in a tower. But Valentina is far from a damsel in distress.

She's slayed her own dragons like the warrior princess she is.

"Can we keep him?"

"Of course we can. You can change his name if you like?"

She mulls over my comment before shaking her head. "I like Cat."

I do too.

There's nothing I want to take with me, so I bid farewell to a place that was never a home and only hope that wherever we're going will be better than here.

We wait in the dining room, but for what, I don't know. But

I trust Valentina, and if she said we're getting out of here, then we're getting out of here. She sits still, patting Cat softly. But I know there is so much going on behind those curious eyes.

We both hear the squeaking of someone's shoes on the linoleum.

Valentina sits upright, watching the doorway intently. But who she sees has her frowning.

One of the sisters is following a tall man. He wears a suit and is groomed immaculately. When he sees Valentina and me, he nods.

"Let's go."

That's it.

He doesn't explain where we're going. Or who he is. Just that we're to follow and no isn't an option.

"Where's Aldo?" Valentina asks, and I assume that's the person who is supposed to save us from this shithole.

The man doesn't reply.

The sister clutches the silver crucifix around her neck. She doesn't have a say in any of this, and I guess she's worried about what Father Merry will say because she didn't seek his permission. He's probably still down for the count.

I don't know who this man is, but going with him is a far better option than staying here, so I stand. He doesn't seem the type who appreciates small talk, so I simply wait for further instruction.

"Come now. She waits," the man says. "My name is Franklin."

"Who is *she*?" Valentina stubbornly argues. "Aldo said he would come."

Franklin peers down his nose at Valentina, clearly annoyed by her rebellion. "I will not ask again."

Before she can protest, I gently cup her elbow and coax her to stand. She allows me to guide her, but I can see her apprehension. We follow Franklin while the sister crosses herself.

I wonder why.

It's like a death march as the sisters who are awake at this ungodly hour stand on the sidelines, watching us as we walk toward the front door. A look of fear mars their faces. I wonder just what awaits us outside these prison walls.

They appear anxious, and I know that's because Father Merry isn't here. Will they be punished for this? I hope so. I hope they never forget Valentina because she deserves to be remembered forever.

The door buzzes open, and I follow Franklin through it but stop when I don't hear Valentina follow.

Turning over my shoulder, I see she's stopped dead in her tracks, clutching Cat to her chest. She appears afraid.

"What if it's worse out there than it is in here?"

I take a moment to ponder her question because we're

literally walking into the unknown.

Valentina doesn't seem to know this man, so we're putting our faith in a stranger. He's not made his intentions clear. But I know for certain that there is no place worse than here.

"Then we fight together," I finally reply, offering her my hand.

She licks her trembling lips.

I don't pity her because I know she would hate such a thing, but I hate that she thinks being locked away in here is a better alternative than living.

She meets my eyes, and all I see is trust in hers as she slowly slips her hand into mine.

I lead her from this hell on earth, and the moment the cool morning breeze slaps our cheeks, I tip my face to the heavens and smile.

We're finally free.

CHAPTER 5

VALENTINA

We've driven for hours.

But I don't mind.

It's sensory overload as I try to keep up with the sights and sounds that flood my brain. I've not seen or heard them before.

Being outside the walls of the orphanage reveals just how much I've missed. Being locked away was safe in a sense because being out here in the big world is terrifying. But as Lenny takes my hand, I know everything will be all right.

I still feel unease because everything is so...new. I didn't realize the world was so big.

Franklin hasn't spoken a word.

He looks at me briefly in the rearview mirror before returning his attention to the road. I wonder if he works for Aldo. That would make sense as the sisters wouldn't allow us to leave unless payment was made.

But I can't shake the feeling that something is amiss.

"Come now. She waits."

Who is she?

Aldo never mentioned a woman.

It seems my questions are about to be answered when the van turns into a driveway. Big steel gates are in front of us, and a security booth is to the left. When the guard inside sees us, he nods at Franklin before pushing a button, and the gates open slowly.

The neighborhood is affluent, but I can't see the house past the thick greenery that shields it from prying eyes. Lenny and I bend low in our seats to get a better look, and when Franklin ascends the driveway, we gasp in utter shock.

As the foliage peels away, a white mansion set on a hill can be seen. The windows are endless as are the stories. The house has balconies coming out from all sides, giving off the appearance of an almost compound.

This is our new home?

The closer we get, the more lavish I can see this place to be.

The lawns are manicured. The water fountain of three musical cherubs adds to the charm. The marbled stairs lead to white double doors.

Just who lives here?

Franklin parks the van and unlocks the doors, indicating we're to get out.

I clutch onto Cat, suddenly more afraid than I've ever been before.

"It's going to be okay."

Lenny's voice calms me, and I nod, realizing I can do this. I didn't come this far to quit.

We step out, the thin soles of my shoes doing nothing to protect my feet from the graveled drive. Lenny stands in front of me, something I noticed he did with Father Merry.

He folds his arms and stares a hole in the front door as we wait for it to open. Franklin also waits, as it seems whoever owns this house demands respect, and when the white doors open, I understand why that is.

She is finally revealed.

Her long hair is blacker than the darkest night. But her eyes are clearer than a cloudless sky. She is slender but not frail. She fills her tall frame with ease. Her nails are bright red as are her lips. Gold jewelry complements her tight black pantsuit.

Just who is this woman?

Her heels click down the stairs as she approaches us. Lenny

doesn't move. He stands tall, protecting me. I appreciate the sentiment, but I don't feel ill at ease with this woman. I don't know why. I just know she isn't going to hurt us.

So I step out from behind him and face the most beautiful woman I've ever seen.

She stops walking when we lock eyes. A look of perhaps surprise on her stunning face. It's gone before I question it.

"Hello," she finally says with an accent similar to Aldo's. "I am Gianna Ricci, your new family. This is your home now."

She doesn't smile, but she isn't unfriendly either. However, her short announcement leaves so many unanswered questions.

"Hello, Gianna," Lenny says confidently. "Not that we're unappreciative, but who are you?"

Gianna has the perfect poker face. "Hello, Lennon. But you prefer to be called Lenny?"

He nods.

"Well, Lenny, all questions will be answered in due time, but for now, let's get you fed, washed, and out of those rags."

She turns, indicating we're to follow.

Franklin waits for us to move. Perhaps he's afraid we'll run. But where would we run to? We're orphans no one wants, so I don't understand why a woman like Gianna would want us. We're useful to her for some reason.

I just don't know what that reason is.

We follow her, and the moment I climb the stairs and get

a glimpse of the foyer, I feel more than undeserving. I kick off my dirty shoes, fearing I'll leave grime on the polished floors. Lenny leaves on his boots and ensures he stays in front of me as he follows Gianna.

She doesn't say a word as she leads us down a long corridor until we reach a door. She opens it. A king-sized bed and other bedroom items adorn this huge space.

"This is your room, Lenny. There is everything you need inside the bathroom. All the clothes inside the cupboard and drawers are yours. You have an hour."

"An hour for what?" he asks, confused.

Gianna simply smiles before turning around and addressing me. "Come."

I look at Lenny, biting my lip, but he nods that it'll be okay.

Without him, I'm afraid, but I eventually follow Gianna because I don't want to get lost.

I hold tightly on to Cat while I take in my surroundings. When we reach the grand staircase with red carpeted stairs, I can't help but take note of how soft the carpet feels beneath my bare feet. The sunlight streaming in from the stained glass windows shoots rainbow spheres across the floor.

I trace them with my toes and wonder if this is what my life will be from now on.

The hallway at the top of the stairs is long, giving me a bird's-eye view of below. It feels as though I'm a princess in her tower, looking at her kingdom below. It's surreal as I only ever saw something like that in the tattered storybooks I stole from the library.

But now, it's as if I am living a real-life fairy tale.

"This is your room," Gianna says, opening a door.

When I hesitate, she moves aside, gesturing for me to go in. But I can't.

"Why are you being so nice to me?"

My question appears to take her off guard. "Would you prefer I be mean to you instead?"

I shake my head.

"Then do not ask stupid questions because you are not a stupid girl."

And just like that, Gianna reveals she doesn't appreciate weakness.

I won't make the same mistake again.

"Good girl. Meet me in the gardens in an hour."

And without another word, she leaves me alone.

I peer into the room, almost afraid to go in, for fear this is one big joke. To be given such luxuries, only for them to be taken away. But I remember Gianna's words and use them to take one step, then two into the bedroom.

It's so big in here, I almost feel lost. I'm not used to such space. The bed is draped in pink silks with a sheer curtain hanging from the wooden posts. I've never seen such a design before.

My feet sink into the plush white carpet as I walk over to the walk-in closet. I see all sorts of clothes hanging from the rails, and when I open the drawers, I find clean socks and underwear.

Are these all for me?

I finger over the garments and decide on a simple white dress. The tag is still attached. I can see it cost a lot of money.

I place Cat onto the floor, and he goes about examining his new home happily. I think he will be happy here. But will I?

Grabbing what clothes I need, I walk into the attached bathroom and take a moment to appreciate its beauty. Everything is so white and clean. So clean it practically sparkles.

The claw tub, although beautiful, drags bad memories to the surface, so I strip off and turn on the faucets in the shower.

I will never take a bath again.

Pushing aside those memories that have no place in my new home, I step into the shower and stand under the hot spray.

It feels wonderful.

Having a shower all to myself is something I can get used to very quickly. I didn't realize a shower could feel this good. I wash myself with the coconut-smelling soap until my fingers are wrinkled, but I don't care because I finally feel clean—in every sense of the word.

I step out and dry myself with the huge fluffy towel.

I dress and take a deep breath before looking at myself in

the mirror.

I don't recognize the person I see.

My cheeks are rosy, and although I am tired, my eyes don't appear afraid.

I look different.

I feel different.

Finding a brush in the top drawer, I comb it through my hair until it's perfectly straight and soft. I don't bother drying it because I'm running out of time.

I quickly brush my teeth.

I slip on my knee-high white socks and Mary Janes with five minutes to spare.

Closing the door so Cat doesn't get out, I realize I have no idea where the gardens are. This is surely a test Gianna laid down for me, and I cannot fail.

Taking the stairs two at a time, I race out the front door because there are gardens out there, but when I don't see Gianna, I take a left and run to the side of the house in hopes she's there.

She's not.

My heart is beating so loudly, I can hear it in my ears, but I don't give up. I continue my search for what feels like hours, and as I run past the inground pool, I hear something catch on the wind.

It's a tiny meow.

I pause and close my eyes, using the sound as my guide, and when I hear it again, I know it's coming from down the hill. I don't think twice and run so fast, the wind blinds me, but I continue going until I see Gianna standing with Lenny near a stream that snakes below the property.

Something is very wrong with Lenny's expression, and I don't know why until I see what Gianna is holding.

The decline is rocky, but I make it down without falling because I've already made a grave error, one in which I'm about to pay dearly for. I slow down and try to compose myself. But it's too late.

Gianna looks at her gold watch. "You're late."

"I know," I breathlessly reply. "I didn't know where the gardens were. I'm sorry. It won't happen again."

Her red lips are pulled into a thin line as she pats Cat. I don't know how she got him, but I do know that this is not good.

"Why do you have Cat?"

Lenny discreetly shakes his head, hinting I'm not to ask questions.

He looks good in his black jeans, boots, and white shirt with a flamingo print. His hair is wet but flicked back like he ran his fingers through it. We both look different, it appears, but what's the same is the fact he is still trying to protect me from the evil that comes.

"Valentina." It's the first time she's said my name. It rolls off her tongue like she's said it before. "I thought we established you were not to ask stupid questions."

I don't know if this is a trick question, so I persevere anyway. "We did, but I do not understand why you have Cat. Forgive me for my foolishness."

She mulls over my comment, patting Cat.

"You are forgiven, but let this be a lesson learned." She passes Cat to Lenny, who looks at her just as confused as I am. "Drown him."

Surely, I misheard her. But it's apparent I did not.

"What?" I cry, running forward, tears streaming down my cheeks.

Lenny clutches Cat to his chest protectively. "No."

Gianna appears taken aback that he disobeyed her. "That wasn't a choice. It was an order."

"I don't take orders from anyone."

She laughs, but nothing about it is kind.

"Please, Gianna, no—"

I don't have a chance to finish before she strikes out and slaps me across the cheek. She slaps me so hard, I taste blood.

Lenny growls, launching forward, but I thrust out a trembling hand, stopping him from lashing out at Gianna.

He thankfully obeys.

"I u-understand. It won't happen again," I say, allowing the blood from the corner of my mouth to trickle down my chin.

This is our first lesson, and we've both failed.

"Good because I do not give second chances. I will not raise weaklings. I need fighters. And if neither of you have brains and brawn, then it's best I return you now."

Return us? That's how easily she can dispose of us.

She needs fighters? For what? Just who is Gianna, and what have Lenny and I walked into?

"We are *not* weak," Lenny says firmly.

"No, you are not. But you love," she replies with disgust. "And that is what makes you weak. *Love* makes you weak. Love will be the death of you. Love does not do anything but hurt. Learn that, and you will survive in this world."

I don't understand any of this.

"What do you want with us?" Lenny doesn't seem to care that Gianna is our judge, jury, and executioner. I admire his strength, and I know that Gianna does too.

Someone like her has done her research. She knows we're the misfits who don't do what we're told. It's a trait that works in her favor but also against her because, like any wild animal, she needs to break us in. And she knows we will fight her every step of the way.

She will take away the things we love to teach us a lesson, and now, I understand why she adopted both Lenny and me. He is the only thing I care about in this world. And I think he feels the same way about me.

We are one another's collateral, and Gianna will use that for her gain.

She doesn't care about our past. About where we came from. She doesn't care what our aspirations are because she only cares about using us for her own personal gain. The question now is, what does she need us for?

"All will be revealed very soon. Until then, don't question me again."

I stand my ground as she walks toward me. I know better than to cower. She uses her thumbs to wipe away my tears.

"Let these be the last of your tears."

And with that, she turns on her heel and leaves us alone.

Thankfully, Cat survived another day. But can the same be said for both Lenny and me?

Once she's out of earshot, Lenny passes me Cat. "It would be kinder to let him fend for himself."

He's right. But I can't abandon him. I won't do to him what my mother did to me.

This is her fault. All of it. And I know here, now, that I will do *anything*. I will kill *anyone* to find her and do to her what she did to me. If Gianna can help me achieve that, then I will do what I am told.

"What does she want with us?"

Lenny shrugs, and for the first time since meeting him, he

genuinely looks concerned.

He too knows that whatever is headed our way can't be good because neither of us will mistake Gianna as the motherly type.

We're here for a reason.

But what's the reason?

I wake to a blaring alarm.

At first, I believe I'm stuck in a nightmare, but when my senses play catch-up, I realize I'm not dreaming.

Rubbing the sleep from my eyes, I look around the room and wonder if perhaps a fire triggered the alarm. But I don't see any smoke.

Placing Cat into the pillowcase for safety, I quickly run to the doorway and peer into the hallway, wondering what's happening.

The alarm continues to blare.

I don't see any commotion, but an alarm wouldn't sound for no reason. Just as I'm about to race to Lenny's room, I see his mussed brown hair bouncing up the stairs.

"Are you okay?" he asks, placing me at arm's distance and peering me over.

I nod, touched by his kindness. "What's going on?"

"I don't know. Let's find out."

He grabs my hand and leads me down the hallway. When we don't see anything up here, we head downstairs. Lenny seems to know his way around, and I guess that's because he's taken the time to investigate.

I don't have time to admire the huge kitchen he drags me through because the alarm picks up speed, producing a panicked, shrill noise. The urgency of his tone has my heart racing because it suddenly feels like we're running out of time.

Lenny opens the back door, which leads to a balcony.

We stop as he peruses over the edge, and when I see Gianna standing in an open field, lit by a floodlight, my stomach drops.

She tips her chin upward, staring right at us.

Lenny doesn't hesitate and drags me down the stairs as the alarm grows more and more urgent. The moment we reach the grassy field, the alarm stops.

I don't know if that's a good or bad thing.

Gianna looks at her watch with a stiff upper lip.

She's dressed in all black. Tight black yoga pants. A black tank. And sneakers. Her long hair is tied into a high ponytail. She looks ready for combat.

"Four minutes and twenty seconds," she says, shaking her head. "It takes thirty-three seconds from your room, Lenny, but I'm guessing the delay is because you used your heart instead of your head."

She looks at me like I'm a helpless bug she could squash under her shoe.

"A lot can happen in four minutes and twenty seconds. The house could be completely swarmed and apprehended in four minutes and twenty seconds."

"Apprehended by who?"

Gianna smiles, the first genuine response I've seen on her face.

"By anyone who wants all of this." She sweeps her hand toward the house. "Everyone is the enemy. Never mistake anyone to be your friend. People will only be good to you because they want something from you, and when they get that, they'll betray you and not feel a thing.

"Don't wait. Never hesitate. You strike first. If you are vulnerable, your enemy will exploit that for their own gain. There is no loyalty. There is no love. That's lesson number two."

First lesson is don't ask stupid questions.

And the second is don't be vulnerable.

"Just what do you want from us?"

I hold my breath, afraid Lenny has broken rule number one.

Gianna smirks. "You are a very clever young man. I will look after you. I will keep you safe. My home will always be yours. You will never go hungry. You will never be afraid."

I hold my breath, waiting for the punchline because there's

a catch. I know there is.

"And what do you expect in return?"

Gianna's red lips tip up into a catlike smirk. "Your undevoted loyalty."

"And?" Lenny prompts, folding his arms across his bare chest.

She doesn't answer.

She turns to look at me and says, "Take off your nightgown."

It's on the tip of my tongue to ask why, but I don't because that would breach both of her rules. It's apparent she sees me as a weakling, so I squash down my embarrassment and slip off the white nightgown over my head.

I have on underwear and a crop top, so I'm not totally naked, but standing bare in front of Lenny has my cheeks blushing. However, I don't cover up. I stand with confidence.

Gianna smiles. It's apparent she's pleased I listened. I don't know why, but her approval makes me happy. I find myself wanting to do it more.

She looks at Lenny. He has his cheek turned, respecting my modesty. I find the sentiment to be kind because no one has ever treated me with such respect before.

But Gianna clearly doesn't when she brings her foot down onto his knee. He buckles but stays upright. He glares at her while she simply dares him with a look to challenge her.

He doesn't.

"Never take your eyes off the enemy," she states, circling him like prey.

"I didn't realize you were."

"Never assume," she counters, stalking him like a lithe cat. "Yet another lesson."

I watch with interest, unsure what's about to happen next.

Lenny soon reads her stance and mirrors her movements. It's kill or be killed, and I suddenly fear how accurate that saying may be.

Gianna clearly knows how to fight. The way she moves, she looks like she can bring a man to his knees with ease. I watch with interest because something inside me stirs in excitement. I want to carry the confidence she does.

"Hit me."

Lenny knows she isn't joking, so he advances and attempts to strike her without hesitation. But Gianna reads his moves with ease and effortlessly dodges his attack. She doesn't give him time to rethink his decision because she bends low and uses an upward sweep of her palm to hit him in the stomach.

He staggers backward, inhaling sharply because she winded him.

He soon recovers and advances with fire behind his eyes. He's mad she was able to catch him unawares. He attempts to connect with her ribs, but she jumps back and kicks him in the flank.

He clutches his side, breathing deeply through his nose.

I can't look away because Gianna isn't breaking a sweat. I've seen Lenny fight, but he doesn't compare to Gianna. She's a beast and makes it look so easy.

He lunges out to strike her, but again, she is too fast and spins in a circle before punching him in the kidneys.

"You disappoint me," she tsks, brushing back a stray hair that has come loose—one single hair while Lenny looks like he's about to pass out. "Perhaps fighting someone a little more in your league then."

She turns to look at me, and I now understand why she asked me to disrobe.

She did this so I would be vulnerable—to Lenny and myself. She thought if I was half naked, then I would be too occupied protecting my modesty to protect myself. And Lenny wouldn't want to hurt me while I was vulnerable this way.

A lesson learned—*if you are vulnerable, your enemy will exploit that for their gain.*

But there is another way to look at it; what if the prey was really the predator in disguise? Could the little lamb fool the Big Bad Wolf into thinking she was nothing but a weakling when, in reality, she was just biding her time, looking for his weaknesses to use against him and play him at his own game?

Only one way to find out…

"I will not fight her," Lenny says, making it clear Gianna

can go to hell.

I whimper, wrapping my arms around my frail frame. Gianna watches me closely. Can she see through my ruse?

"It's okay, I won't hurt you," Lenny says, walking toward me, only offering me comfort.

This is wrong, and I know it is. Lenny has been nothing but nice to me. To betray him this way leaves me riddled with guilt. But I have this urge to please Gianna. Or perhaps I have something to prove.

I've been the underdog my entire life, and now, I can change that, but it's at the expense of my only friend. What sort of person does that make me?

Lenny has been there for me when no one else ever has, and now, I plan on exploiting his trust.

What do I do?

The closer he gets, the louder my heart beats. I don't think I can.

I suddenly feel light on my feet. This is not the person I want to be. I don't want to be someone who treats people this way, especially Lenny.

But I'm also sick of being weak.

I refuse to be feeble a second longer.

The way Gianna was able to protect herself is what I want. No more being at the mercy of vile men like Father Merry. Or his friends.

No more.

I'm done being a victim.

I will sacrifice who I must to never be at the mercy of anyone ever again.

I sniff back my staged tears as I push out my bottom lip.

Lenny's face softens.

My heart breaks.

The moment he reaches out for me, I think of my mother— the faceless woman who never gave me a chance. She had borne me into this world only to abandon me.

What sort of a person does that?

And my father, nothing but an animal.

What hope was there for me? With two parents such as mine, was I always destined to be this way?

Perhaps that is why Father Merry singled me out. Did he sense I was the root of evil and only fated to commit horrific acts in the vein of my father and mother?

Did I deserve the acts bestowed on me?

As a flash of light strikes the heavens, I realize that no, this isn't my fault. I didn't deserve what was done to me, and I'll be damned if I let those who hurt me dictate my life a second longer.

I am not weak.

I'm a survivor.

I could have given up, but I didn't.

And I promise here and now, under the starless sky, that those who wronged me will pay. But first, I need to think with my head and not my heart. Because if you can fight the one you love and beat them…then you can fight anyone.

"It's okay," Lenny says once again, kindness swimming in those vibrant eyes.

I take his hand and relish this moment of warmth because I'm certain it will be my last. The moment is soon replaced with fire when I remember all the horrible things I've endured, and I thrive on that to draw Lenny toward me, catching him unawares.

He underestimated me—he won't ever do that again.

No one will.

"I'd never hurt y—"

Before he has a chance to break my heart further, I finish this quick. I don't want to delay gratification. It hurts too much. I won't win fighting him, so I draw my knee up and connect with what's between his legs.

His eyes widen, clearly stunned, before he drops to the ground, wheezing for air.

I take no pleasure in seeing him in pain, but as I turn to look at Gianna, I see that she does—or rather, she is pleased I did what she said.

"Good, *piccola*. What did you learn?"

I think over her question because I know this too is part of her test.

Lenny has gotten up but is sure to stand far away. I don't blame him. The betrayal he feels is written all over his face. I know this changes everything between us now.

Is that what Gianna wanted all along?

But I need him to know why I did what I did, and maybe he can find it in his heart to forgive. Or, at the very least, understand my actions.

With eyes locked with his, I reply, "If you can fight the one you…love and beat them…then you can fight anyone."

Gianna nods while my confession only seems to incite Lenny further.

"Very good. We will meet again tomorrow morning at nine o'clock." Gianna leaves me alone with Lenny, who doesn't say a word.

We simply stare at one another, and although I'm saddened that Lenny looks at me with hatred in his eyes, I don't regret what I did. It's either eat or be eaten, and I soon realize that I would, that I *have* betrayed the one I love.

"Daddy's proud, baby girl."

That voice is familiar.

But why?

It comforts but disturbs me all in the same breath, and the fact eludes that I just heard my father's voice.

I don't know if it's his, or maybe I have finally succumbed to the voices inside my head. Regardless, I know that I was reborn tonight.

I was reborn into who I was always destined to become.

CHAPTER 6

VALENTINA
SEVENTEEN YEARS OLD

"*Ci stai provando?*"

Franklin doesn't appreciate my sass and charges toward me, swinging his sword like he's in some B-grade martial arts movie. But like always, he fails to connect with me as I easily dodge him.

"Too slow, old man."

Insult someone's pride—works like a charm.

He should know better. He's been my sparring partner for years. He's taught me all I know. But the thing he never anticipated was that I would eventually outfight him.

I came here a broken, scared little girl, a *piccola* as Gianna still calls me, but now, I'm an uncontrollable force that will stop at nothing to get what I want.

And what I want is a simple request.

What I want is to find my mother. I don't know what I would say to her when I do, though. I guess I just want to look at her eyes…look her in the eye as I cut out her heart, just as she did to me.

I'm not being melodramatic. Thanks to Franklin, I know how to do such things.

The second thing is to burn Saint Maria's Orphanage to the ground, but not before torturing Father Merry in the most creative of ways.

Again, thanks to Franklin, I can give a man a very artistic Colombian necktie in ten seconds.

But I would savor my time with Father Merry just as he did with me. Just the thought has my body tingling in excitement.

Once upon a time, these things were my main reasons for enduring the tests Gianna laid down for me. For years, she fed me. She schooled me. And in return, she pushed me to my breaking point—until I no longer could feel my body physically and metaphorically because her grand plan was soon to be revealed.

She adopted me all those years ago for one purpose and

one purpose only—to be a killer.

I'm Gianna's secret weapon. No one suspects a young girl to be able to do what I've been trained to do. However, I wait for her to reveal my purpose in her grand scheme because I know she has something big planned.

I say I'm ready.

But she says that I'm not.

So I wait.

I train.

And this is the reason I stay here. I cannot go until I get what I want.

And pay no heed to the longing I feel whenever *he* ignores me, which is all the time.

This brings me to my last and most important want.

Lennon Shepherd.

But he would rather slit his own throat than talk to me ever again.

That night all those years ago changed everything.

The boy can hold a damn grudge. But I know it's more than that.

He felt betrayed. He put his trust in me—something he's not done since—and in return, I made an example out of his compassion, making him appear weak, which Gianna despises.

That day changed things for me as she didn't look at me like a feeble young girl. She saw my spirit and trained me accordingly.

She trained us both.

But day by day, he slipped further and further away from me and before long, I only ever saw him when we trained.

He made clear we would never be what we once were. And I was the one to blame.

I try not to care, but when I see him, I know I'm fooling myself because I care. I care a lot.

Lenny is now eighteen years old.

He has always been attractive, but he has grown into himself and no longer is the boy I once knew.

Lennon Shepherd is all alpha man.

His mussed brown hair is long on top with shorter sides. The longer strands of hair fall in just the right way, framing his chiseled face, a face I usually want to slap as he lifts those full lips into a knowing smirk when he catches me watching him.

He always seems to have a five-o'clock shadow. Never clean-shaven, which just adds to his bad-boy vibe.

His arms are inked. The pieces on his body are well-thought-out and map imperative events, objects, and times in his life that impacted him.

He's literally a work of art.

To complete that perfection, he has a silver hooped nose ring that just seems to accentuate that strong, perfect nose.

His style is typical Lenny—Hawaiian shirt with the buttons

halfway done up to expose that broad chest, ripped black jeans, silver rings and chunky linked bracelets, and boots. Something which sounds so simple looks anything but on Lenny, and that's because of the attitude he sports. He turns heads the moment he enters the room.

He knows it.

The girls he's snuck into the house also know it.

The thought of those girls has images of them floating in the pool, belly-up, crashing into me, and a giggle slips past my lips.

On cue, just like always, the sound alerts Lenny, and he turns to look at me.

He may hate me, but the connection we've had since the moment we met still runs strong. Most days, the angst between us makes me want to kiss and slap those cheeks.

When our eyes lock, he looks at me how he always does—with the perfect poker face.

His expression doesn't change.

He gives me absolutely nothing.

And I hate him for it.

How can he be so unaffected by me? While I am burning up inside.

The sun catches the compass pendant from his neck. I wonder if he's found what he's looking for. His shirt seems to be unbuttoned more so than usual, revealing a tanned expanse of his broad chest. I know what he's packing beneath that shirt.

His body is that of a fighter—lean and muscled.

That, coupled with a face carved by the devil himself and not many can withstand the charms of Lennon Shepherd.

And boy, does he know it.

"Messa a fuoco!" Franklin yells and takes advantage of my daydreaming as he rams the butt of the sword into my stomach, winding me.

"Motherfucker," I curse under my breath, directing my curse at Lenny, who pulls a sarcastic pained face before walking inside.

"You know better, *bambina.*"

Franklin has been a father figure to me, which is the only reason I allow his term of endearment. If anyone else were to call me this, I would cut out their tongue.

"I hate him."

"Good, use that anger in how you know."

He's right.

Picking up my sword, I circle Franklin, and all is right in the world once again.

I may be a skilled fighter, but matters of the heart? Gianna has failed to teach me how to fight that battle and win.

Franklin and I train until my body aches and sweat coats every inch of my flesh. But the pain makes me feel alive.

Just as I trip him and place the tip of my blade to the hollow of his throat, Gianna appears. Like always, I didn't hear her approach, another thing she taught me.

Light on my feet, but heavy as I swing my blade.

"Very good, *piccola*, but watch your footing."

Before I can argue that nothing is wrong with my footing, she bends low and sweeps her leg out, tripping me over. I land near Franklin on the grass. I don't bother getting up.

Her face appears above me, smiling in victory.

She's just as striking as she was the first moment we met. And just as deadly.

During my years here, I've learned very little about her. She holds her cards close to her chest. I never pushed because I learned early on that Gianna doesn't do emotion.

Her face is beautiful, but it's a mask because beneath that facade lays such malice. She is unfeeling. And I fear I am now too.

She has educated me, and thanks to her, I'm a good pupil in both education and martial arts.

But I am still very much a naive girl for everything in between.

I think back to the kind man, Aldo. All those years ago, he was the one who was supposed to be my savior, but Gianna took me instead.

I wonder what happened to him.

From being unwanted since I was born to having two people

want me; something is not right. But I cannot ask Gianna. I wouldn't get an answer, so I don't waste my breath. But I can't help but wonder why she adopted me instead.

"Get up. We're going out," she says, offering me her hand.

I know better than to accept.

I stand of my own accord, dusting myself off.

Another rule of Gianna's—cleanliness is next to godliness.

"You look a fright. Go get cleaned up. I will call for you in an hour."

She turns to leave with no further explanation.

Leaving the house is not a common occurrence, especially at night.

But I know better than to argue because when Gianna speaks, it's an order.

My fingers glide over the silk ruffles of my ball gown.

It's hard to believe this is me who stands in front of the mirror. I've never worn anything like this before. But when I entered my room and saw the red dress on the bed, it was clear Gianna had something big planned.

She gave me no direction on how I was to present myself. She never has.

What I see on TV about girls my age getting ready for

milestone events such as prom or birthdays is so foreign to me.

They look so happy.

Their smiles are so big.

But I can't feel what they do because I do not know how.

I know something is wrong with me. Perhaps I'm broken to be without feeling.

But when I see them laugh and cry, I feel absolutely nothing. I want to experience this rainbow of emotions, but I cannot.

I step closer to the mirror, leaning forward so my face is inches away. I burst into staged laughter, wiping away my imaginary tears. I force myself to feel…something.

But I don't.

I use my fingers to tip my mouth into a wide grin, hoping to express something remotely human.

But I look like a fraud.

Only when I release my mouth do I feel myself.

I've not mingled with peers because I've been homeschooled. I don't leave the house because I have everything I need here. I don't have any friends, bar Cat, but that's by choice because I dislike people. I watch them on TV, and their exchanges look like so much work.

I don't know how to laugh and gossip about boys or do makeup because I just don't care about trivial things that mean nothing to me.

The friendships I read about or watch play out in movies

seem so fake. There's so much drama, and all for what? From what I can see, most people don't like each other and only formulate friendships because it seems to be society's way of acceptance.

I don't want to fit in.

I just want to be me.

If that makes me a freak or a weirdo, then I would rather that than be someone I am not.

My long brown hair is loose, and my makeup is light.

I have Gianna to thank for my simplicity. She is the most beautiful woman I have ever seen, and she is without makeup or fancy hairdos.

Her confidence is all the wardrobe she needs.

The strapless red dress has a sweetheart neckline that pinches at the waist before ballooning into many layers of tulle.

It's rather extravagant, making me wonder where we're going.

I have two minutes to spare as I slip on my heeled knee-high boots. With nowhere to carry my blade, I have hidden it inside.

I'm always prepared for battle—another lesson learned.

I make my way down the staircase, head held high regardless of the fact the heels hurt my feet. But in pain comes discipline, so I focus on that because I have a feeling a lot more pain is to be had tonight.

And that's confirmed when Lenny appears at the bottom of the staircase. He wears a black suit. White shirt. Black bow tie. A red rose is pinned to the silk lapel of his jacket.

When he sees me, something happens that hasn't happened in a very long time—his poker face slips, and I see something other than hate behind those blue-gray eyes.

It's soon gone when I ascend the last stair.

He doesn't speak.

Neither do I.

We simply stand and wait for further command.

Even though we don't speak, we never have an uncomfortable silence. It doesn't make sense, but there is comfort in the silence.

I focus on something other than his scent. He always smells good. I often smell him before I see him. It's a Lenny thing.

But his mouthwatering fragrance can go to hell when he mutters under his breath, "There *is* a girl hidden underneath there after all."

"Fuck you," I counter, refusing to look at him.

"Aw, sorry, my bad. I was mistaken."

"Go fu—"

"Enough," Gianna says, entering the foyer.

She appears breathtaking in a fitted white gown.

She looks me over and gives nothing away. I wonder if she approves.

She rearranges the necklines to expose more of my ample

cleavage. She brushes back my hair. There is no love to her touch, though. She uses me as a pawn in whatever game she soon plays.

When she looks down at my feet, I lift my skirt to reveal my shoes.

Even though they are dressy boots with a bow and zip, she understands why I chose these instead of heels.

"Perhaps you will survive the night after all."

Her comment isn't made for shock value—she means it.

I don't react, though, because unlike the girls my age who respond to normal events with happiness and excitement, this *is* my normal. The thought of being in danger is *my* happiness and excitement.

She leads the way, and we follow her out the front door.

It's a warm summer evening. Magic is in the air.

A large black luxury car awaits us. We step in, and the driver takes us toward the unknown.

Bach plays softly over the speakers. None of us talk.

Lenny peers out the window. I wonder what he sees.

He could leave at any time, yet he returns. I wonder why. He is of legal age to thrive on his own. He has his choice of girls to start a future. But he stays. I once hoped it was because of me. But that whimsical nonsense was forgotten long ago.

The prospect of being in danger excites me. It's the only time I feel alive.

What would Dr. Phil say?

The drive is long, but I'm not anxious. Gianna has taught me that all good things come to those who wait.

Like all good predators, we must wait for the perfect moment to strike. Premature action can be costly, and there is no room for error.

We arrive at a large white mansion lit up by lights. A party is being held within the extravagant walls. Many expensive cars are parked outside, and the guests who arrive wear nothing but the finest threads.

Our driver pulls up behind a line of cars.

Gianna adjusts her pearls and exhales softly. "Italian only."

Both Lenny and I are fluent, thanks to her teachings.

We both nod.

She doesn't say another word as she exits the car. We follow, knowing better than to ask questions.

Being out in the "real world" is still foreign to me. I've taken comfort in being inside my home because I never had a desire to see what was outside the walls. I've been out there, and all it did was cause me pain.

But being here now, among all these people, I wonder if perhaps I've missed out on all these years.

All the teachings I've learned have been through books and Gianna. I never felt disadvantaged. But was that because Gianna taught me that she was all I needed to survive?

I quash down such thoughts because I don't like them. Despite Gianna's detachment, she has still been the kindest human. I accept what she offers because a starving dog always does.

Another lesson she taught.

But as I look around, I realize that perhaps I only starve because she never feeds me enough. I took what she offered and appreciated it because I had nothing else. But I guess any meal appears appealing if you're always hungry, and I'm always hungry for more.

Lenny towers over the men double his age here, and I notice the heads of many women turning as he passes them. I barely suppress the urge to snap their necks.

Gianna air-kisses the cheeks of a man who smiles, but it's not a pleasant gesture. It's that of a predator, one I have seen before.

He does not recognize me.

But I recognize him.

He sat at that poker table the night I met Aldo. But unlike Aldo, he is a bad man, one who was there to engage in illicit acts against children who needed his protection, not his vile hands on their innocent bodies.

"You're always full of surprises," he says, eyeing me hungrily.

I'm going to rip out his eyes and feed them to him.

Just as I step forward, fingers wrap around my wrist, fingers

I've not felt in a very long time.

The electricity radiating from Lenny's touch will surely set me on fire. He has read me better than I thought, but I shouldn't be surprised. He's always known me better than I've known myself.

The move was discreet, so no one saw. Well, no one but Gianna.

This is a test, and I failed.

It won't happen again.

Subtly removing myself from Lenny's grip, I smile and fake innocence, just as any normal young girl would.

The man makes clear what he wants, and when he whispers something in Gianna's ear, she looks at me as if weighing over his request.

Eventually, she nods.

The man steps forward.

The smell of cigars and heavy-handed cologne brings me back in time.

He loops his arm through mine, escorting me away.

I don't turn away, but I hear something which warms my heart.

"You cannot fight her battles," Gianna says in Italian.

Lenny tried to help me, and I need to prove to him that I don't need his help. I don't need anyone.

Confidence courses through me, and I allow this asshole to

believe I'm his willing fuck doll to do with what he wills.

I don't care if he is Gianna's friend.

I don't care if this is his grand home and this is his lush affair.

And that's because I don't care—period.

I'm so broken; I don't think I can ever be repaired.

So tonight, he dies—and dies by my hand.

My first kill…

Is this why Gianna brought me here? Dressed me in the fanciest silks to take the life of a man who deserves to be dead?

We ascend the staircase, and it disgusts me that no one seems to care when a man escorts a girl half his age upstairs. Perhaps this is because they're just as vile as he.

We walk down a long hallway, and I admire a marble statue of a cherub playing a harp. So pretty. Such pretties disguise what lurks behind this wealth.

He opens a door. A very extravagant bedroom is behind the white door.

We step inside, and I smell the same cologne he wears. This is his room.

He closes the door and leans against it with a grin.

He takes his time examining me, making no secret of what he's thinking. The look reminds me of all the times I was brought down to that basement. Of all the times my body was desecrated in a place that should have been holy.

"You don't understand English?"

I simply smile.

I wonder if he knows Aldo. I want to ask, but I cannot. I need to just exist.

He pushes off the door, raising his hands like he means no harm. But I know what those hands can do. "We're just going to have some fun," he says, but clucks his tongue. "Don't know why I'm bothering. You can't understand a fucking word I'm saying."

He laughs.

I continue to smile.

The closer he gets, the more intense the memories invade my mind.

Squeak...

Squeak, squeak...

Squeak, squeak, squeak...

Was it his turn once his friend had finished?

"We can't save them all."

That's what Aldo said to me, and he was right.

In this world, we can only save ourselves.

The asshole stands in front of me. He looks like any man you'd pass on the street. He doesn't look like a monster, a vile beast mothers warn their children about. And it's because of this fact that he is the most dangerous monster of all.

But at this moment, I realize that so am I.

He underestimated me because, to him, all I am is a pretty prize, which is why Gianna dressed me this way. Looks can be deceiving, and in this asshole's case, he is about to be betrayed in the most violent of ways.

He brushes the backs of his fingers along my chest, watching for any cues.

I continue smiling.

"Good girl," he hums, leaning forward and planting a kiss on the side of my throat. "You smell like strawberries. I bet you're ripe for the picking."

Vomit rises because who the fuck speaks this way? Is it supposed to be romantic? I don't know because I don't do romance, but I can't imagine anyone would care to be compared to a fruit.

In this instance, I don't understand a word he is saying.

His kisses trickle down my neck and over the tops of my breasts. He reaches around and unzips my dress. I stand completely still.

When my dress pools by my feet, he stands back and looks at me.

I'm in a black strapless bra and matching underwear.

"So innocent," he mistakenly says because he has just revealed that he sees me as no threat.

What an idiot.

He rubs over the front of his pants, his dick swelling.

Gianna had a good mind to teach me the difference between men and women and all the sex talk which a child is to learn to keep them safe against men like this *stronzo*.

But my safety was breached long ago.

He unzips his pants and withdraws his hard cock. He begins stroking it before beckoning me with the other hand.

I fake nervousness as I walk over.

He plants a hand on top of my shoulder, forcing me to my knees. He grips my chin and opens my mouth wide.

"Have you sucked dick before?"

"Fuck you, you filthy swine," I sweetly say in Italian.

"I bet those big cocksucking lips have made many men come."

Is this the only thing men think women are good for?

In the movies, in books I read, men do not speak to women this way. But is that make-believe? This is real life, and all I've ever experienced in this lifetime is men who use and abuse women for their own perverted needs.

"Come now, I don't have all night."

He draws my face toward his crotch, his fingers still forcing my mouth open. I have no other choice.

The moment he hits the back of my throat, memories assault me, and I squeeze my eyes shut. I wish to erase them forever and not have them a part of me.

But they are.

They'll never leave me.

They make up who I am, and I realize I must use that as fuel to take back what was stolen from me.

He uses my hair as reins to roughly direct the tempo, and when he pulls out, only to shove himself back into my mouth, I gag.

"Daddy's good girl!" he hollers in delight.

But his comment triggers something in me. It reminds me of who I am. Who I am a spawn of.

Half sinner.

Half saint.

And now, I *am* Daddy's girl as I reach for the knife in my boot.

This bastard is too lost to his pleasure to realize what I'm doing as I suddenly pull back. He looks down, a look of annoyance plastered on his face, but that soon turns to horror when he watches me ram the knife into his cock.

A stunned breath leaves him, which will be one of the last he takes as I stab him in the crotch over and over again. Blood squirts from the wound, showering my face and upper body.

The bloodlust soon rouses the demons inside me, and I happily dance with them as I slice off his cock.

A wheeze slips past his lips as he drops to both knees, grabbing his dickless crotch.

"Bad dog," I mock in English as I want him to know I've

been privy to this charade the entire time.

I slap his cheeks with his severed dick before tossing it over my shoulder like the garbage that it is.

"Please, no, I have a wife and kids."

I'm not sure why he shared this information with me. Was he thinking of them when he forced himself down my throat?

He appears to be in shock while I, still on my knees in front of him, do as I wanted to—I stab my knife into his eyeballs and remove each one with ease.

Anything is easy if you know what you're doing. All you need to do is cut the optic nerve, and that sucker will pop out like an avocado pip.

I suddenly burst into laughter at the analogy.

"Open up," I say, slapping his cheek, and as he wheezes, I toss his eyeballs into his mouth and shove them down his throat with two fingers.

He collapses onto his side as he is now the one to gag.

I slowly stand, looking at my handiwork with pride.

I know I should feel disgust for what I've done.

But I don't.

I'm hungry for more.

The door bursts open, snapping me from my bloodlust state. I turn and see Lenny.

"Hi." I wave with the bloody knife in hand, smiling wide.

"Hi," he finally replies, closing the door behind him.

He looks around the room as if surveying for danger, but doesn't he realize that I'm the threat?

"What a mess you have made, *tesoro mio*," he says, and his term of endearment catches me off guard.

"It's not a mess," I counter, dropping to one knee and yanking on the hair of the man who is on the brink of death. "It's fucking art."

I allow Lenny to see me for who I am as I slash my knife across the man's throat and watch blood spurt from the wound. I watch the life drain from him and feel nothing. Only when he takes his last breath do I stand, but not before spitting on his corpse.

Lenny stands by my side.

The silence envelops us once again.

But I realize this is the first time he's spoken to me without hatred. Actually acknowledged me. Is this what I have to do to repair the damage I did?

He links his fingers through mine, and I allow him to lead me to the en suite. He directs me to sit on the toilet, and I watch as he reaches for a washcloth and runs it under the water. Once it's wet, he begins washing my face and chest with it.

The warmth feels heavenly, which is ironic, considering what he's washing away.

He runs the washcloth under the water many times and meticulously cleans me. The gesture does something to me.

It fills my heart with something other than hate. Perhaps I'm not dead inside after all?

Once I'm clean, he coaxes me to stand.

I open my eyes and accept the mouthwash he offers. I gargle, and when I spit it into the sink, I'm thankful I can no longer taste him in my mouth.

Peering at myself in the mirror, I don't look any different even though I am.

I just killed a man, a man who hurt others. A man who would have hurt me.

Does that make his death okay?

I grapple with that moral question as Lenny returns with my dress in hand.

I didn't even hear him leave.

I redress and look exactly how I did before I entered this room. But nothing is the same inside. I don't know if I passed Gianna's test, but honestly, I don't care. I'll deal with the consequences and accept whatever punishment comes my way.

Lenny grips me by the shoulders and spins me to face him.

He is so much taller than I am.

But I don't feel fragile in his presence, and that's because he knows the damage I can cause.

He's seen it.

But what he does next, I don't understand.

The blood.

The violence.

The fury.

I do.

But as he presses his lips to mine, I cannot comprehend the feelings swimming inside my heart.

It hurts, akin to being kicked in the chest.

It also leaves me breathless.

But the pain—it hurts so good.

He pulls away slowly, and the kiss is chaste. I don't understand why he did this. He reads my confusion as he runs his thumb across the apple of my cheek.

"I want you to remember this night for something else."

Kiss and kill…

Kill and kiss…

My first kiss.

My first kill.

And I don't know what's worse.

His words touch me because he would rather replace the violence with something tender. He knows this changes everything. But is he attempting to save me before I am lost forevermore?

I don't make a fuss and nod.

But little does Lenny know, he saved me long ago.

CHAPTER 7

LENNY

There is so much fucking blood.

Most would be terrified of the girl in front of me, but to me, Valentina is a fucking goddess, slathered in her enemy's blood.

I've never seen her as a sister. And Gianna never raised us this way for a reason. She will wage a war between us one day and use us for her own personal gain. I don't trust her, but Valentina does.

And that is why I have stayed away.

I cannot grow too close to her because, in the end, it'll

destroy us both.

Gianna is right—love makes you weak. Having someone you would die for is collateral. So I detach as best I can even though it kills me to know that Valentina doesn't think I care.

It's because I do care that I pretend she doesn't exist.

But tonight, I could not.

Gianna will no doubt be pissed I snuck away, but the thought of Valentina being here alone, with this motherfucker; I just couldn't deal.

But I should have known she could take care of herself.

However, walking into the carnage I did was something I did not expect.

She is broken, and I'm afraid that perhaps she is too far gone. So much has happened to her. She has known nothing but hate.

And that is why I kissed her because I wanted to replace the memories of her first kill with her first kiss instead.

Kiss or kill.

Kill or kiss.

Both have the ability to destroy one forevermore. I just hope that maybe she'll clutch on to the small shred of light and not be consumed by the darkness eating away at her.

I'm an adult. I can leave at any time. But I don't, and that's because I can't leave Valentina. The need to protect her, which was ingrained in me from the moment we met, hasn't gone away. It's only grown.

So I stay.

I watch from afar, ensuring she's okay.

She thinks I don't care.

But it's because I care that I do what I do.

Gianna adopting us was never by chance. She trained us to be her lapdogs because she is waging a war, and that war… Gianna Ricci is the biggest drug lord this side of the world has ever seen, and her competition is Aldo Cattaneo, the man who Valentina said was coming to "save" us.

Gianna got to us before he could. If he wanted us, then she believed us to be valuable, no doubt. She didn't adopt us out of the goodness of her heart. She did so because her enemy wanted us.

The question to all this, however, is why?

For years, I've been trying to find the answers, but the world's biggest drug lords do not leave paper trails. They don't set a foot out of place.

They have people like Valentina and me doing their dirty work.

We're nothing but pawns to them, which is why I have to be careful.

I am a one-man army because I can only trust myself. I cannot go to Aldo just yet. I need to earn his trust, and the only way I can do that is to betray Gianna. But if I do that, then what happens to Valentina?

So Gianna was right—love does indeed make you weak, but as I look at the beautiful angel in front of me, I would happily surrender to it all because all that we have is love.

"Let's go," I say, gesturing with my head that we're to bounce.

She looks disappointed but nods.

I don't hold her hand.

I step over the corpse, not bothering to conceal the crime. I feel sorry for the poor asshole who has to clean this up because my girl made a mess.

Valentina stops to look at her handiwork with a smile. She curses him out in Italian before following me out the door.

The hallway is empty, but from the ruckus downstairs, the party is still in full swing. When I feel Valentina tug on my wrist, I ignore the fire burning in my belly and yank my arm from her grip.

She appears wounded by my response.

Good.

I turn to look at her, but she catches me off guard as she stands on her toes and reaches up, wiping her thumb across my cheek. I watch as she then smudges a bloodstain down a cherub statue's face. I cleaned her up but failed to do the same to myself.

I see the significance of this because it's something she's done before.

She's done this to *my* face before.

The bloodlust between us is a heady feeling, and I instantly feel myself getting hard.

Seems we're just as fucked up as the other, but it's all we've known.

Once she's done, she gestures I'm to lead the way.

We descend the stairs and are greeted by drunken bodies, laughing obnoxiously, oblivious to the reality in which they exist.

Gianna is not one of these people, however. She sees us before we do her. She's always two steps ahead. And that's why I'm careful.

Without a doubt, she's done her research on us. She knows where my brother is, and it's why I have to play nice when, in reality, I want to bring down her empire and save Valentina from burning alive.

Valentina's bravado simmers when Gianna gives her a knowing look. This is why I need to stay. Gianna is the marionette and Valentina her puppet.

Valentina is Gianna's secret weapon.

Look what she was able to achieve upstairs. Everyone is unsuspecting of a young woman, which Gianna tends to exploit. And the woman Valentina is growing into—no man or woman stands a chance against her.

She is so beautiful. Anyone would happily take their last

breath if her lips delivered the blood kiss.

The thought of another man kissing that mouth has a feral possession overcoming me, and when a fucker walks a little close to Valentina, eyeing her disrespectfully, I don't hide the fact he has three seconds to fuck off before I strangle him with his red bow tie.

Gianna walks, and we're to follow as always—like her little lapdogs.

We slip out into the night, undetected, leaving behind a bloodbath which is the reason we came.

When in the car, we wait for Gianna to speak.

"Your first kill at seventeen," she says with an almost gratification to her tone. "I'm proud of you."

I conceal my anger while Valentina's face expresses her happiness at Gianna's approval. She is never proud, so when moments like this arise, it is as if Valentina cured fucking cancer.

Every move of Gianna's is calculated. She is paving the path for her succession to overthrow her rival and become queen.

"You remember that man?"

Valentina nods.

"How did that make you feel?"

We know better than to make Gianna wait when she asks a question.

"Alive."

I want to open this door and throw us from the car. I

would rather those odds of survival than another moment with Gianna.

Valentina believes it's her I despise when, in reality, I cannot stand being around Gianna. I've had to stop myself countless times from suffocating her in her sleep. Or poisoning her food. But it's fruitless because she doesn't trust me. She watches me, waiting for me to slip up.

I need to catch her unawares. I need to find *her* weakness because we all have one.

And Gianna knows Valentina is mine.

When I find what her weakness is, only then can I leave behind this life and take Valentina—kicking and screaming if I must.

"I knew you were special," she has the gall to say.

She's really tugging on the heartstrings. I have a feeling that's all for me because she knows I see through her bullshit. She has always purposely put us against one another while she stands back and watches the mess she made.

I need to find Aldo, and I need to find him now.

"You're ready."

Both Valentina and I look at Gianna.

Ready for what exactly?

She leaves the statement hanging, of course, because she is a narcissistic asshole.

I thought I had time, but it's clear I don't. I had hoped

Valentina would see what I did, but the point of tonight was to "reward" Valentina. Gianna gave her, her revenge, and now Valentina feels some sense of obligation toward her.

She is building her up for the grand prize, however, and that prize—can you guess what, or rather, who that is?

Ding! Ding! Ding!

Father Merry.

He is the reason Valentina could kill a man with a smile. He is the reason she suffered in ways no child ever should, and I think she has this idea that if she does to him what he did to her, things will be…better.

But there's no better.

Once he's gone, the pain she carries will still be there. It will only create a bigger void, and I fear she will forever be lost in the darkness.

But I won't allow it.

I may not have found Gianna's weakness, but I know one thing she wants—me.

I see the way she watches me. I know I'm no ugly duckling, not that that even fucking matters. You can be the most beautiful person on the outside, but if you're ugly on the inside, you're a fucking impostor. A fake. But I use what I know Gianna likes to hopefully play her at her own game.

When I got my first tattoo of a tree, starting from my shoulder and wrapping its way around my bicep, I saw how she looked at me with lust in her eyes, and I knew I could use that for my gain. So it was then that I decided to become a predator, using what I have to trick people into getting what I want.

And it was so easy.

I usually grab the first thing that's clean, but it works somehow. The pendant around my neck is the only thing that means something to me.

It was my father's, and I ripped it from his throat as he lay dying, begging for help. My mother had taken her last breath long ago. Her corpse beside him. And my baby brother, sitting in the corner of the room with a grin, the bloody hammer he used on them still in his hand.

I had no other choice but to burn the house to the ground, concealing what he had done.

But he wasn't a bad kid. He'd just had enough. I didn't know what they were doing because I was never home. But when he told me, it was too late.

My father wasn't his biological dad, and he made sure Lewis knew this each time he beat him until he was black and blue. And my mom, she didn't do a damn thing about it.

Parents are supposed to protect their kids from the monsters—not be one.

We had no family to stay with, so we were put into the system even though I was promised we wouldn't be separated.

But again, humanity failed.

Not a day passes when I don't think about him. I wonder where he is and if he's safe. And there isn't a day when I don't regret failing him.

I couldn't save the only person who loved me. Not because he had to but because he wanted to.

And that's why I won't allow it to happen again.

I will protect Valentina how I couldn't protect my brother.

We ride the rest of the way in silence, but my mind races.

What is headed Valentina's way?

Gianna has been training us harder and harder, preparing us for something.

But what?

When we pull up at the house, I open the door before the car has come to a stop and get out.

I need to get away from Gianna before I strangle her.

The easy thing would be to ask Gianna, again, where my brother is. She knows. She says she doesn't, but we both know she's lying. And that's why I don't trust her.

That's the reason I'm going to take her down.

She's right because love is collateral. But for someone to use it against you shows that they don't give a fuck about love.

For years, I've tolerated her shit, but it's getting harder and harder. And now that I know something is on the horizon for us, I need to step it up.

I just don't know how.

I have a few ways, but all mean hurting Valentina.

Storming down the hill, I yank off my jacket and throw it to the ground. I do the same with my bow tie. I unbutton three buttons because I suddenly feel like I'm suffocating.

"Fuck," I mutter under my breath, fisting my hair.

I have never felt more helpless.

"What's wrong?"

It takes every ounce of strength I have not to tell her the truth. That I don't trust Gianna and we need to leave this place right now. I don't tell her this because I know what the answer will be, especially after tonight.

So I push aside my emotions and do what I do best—ignore her.

But she does something she's not done before. She grabs my wrist, stopping me from storming off.

I tongue my cheek, making a point to look at her fingers around me. "Did I tell you, you could touch me?"

I attempt to snatch back my arm, but she uses the other hand to hold my forearm. "Did I tell you, you could kiss me?"

Touché, tesoro mio...

I mull over her comment, faking confusion. "We kissed?"

My comment stings, especially since it was her first kiss.

"Oh, fuck you, Lennon."

She only uses my full name when she's angry—like right now.

"I know you dream of that every night."

"How dare you do this?"

"Do what?"

When she takes her time, I yawn, which infuriates her further.

She releases me only to do something which shocks but pisses me off in the same breath—she slaps me.

I can see the surprise on her face, but she soon owns it. "Oops, I slipped."

Every part of me demands I walk away, but that animalistic part of me that is all alpha dog just can't.

She knows she has a three-second window before I make her regret coming out here to see if I was okay.

She turns, but it's too late.

I pick her up and throw her over my shoulder. She fights wildly, but I hold her tight. She weighs next to nothing, but she puts up a good fight.

"Put me down, or I swear to God—"

As she flails uncontrollably, I buck her off-balance, and she grips me for support. Her threats go ignored, however, as I continue walking.

"Can't keep your hands off me, *tesoro mio?*"

"Oh, get over yourself! And I am not your *tesoro mio.*"

"You are what I say you are."

A string of Italian profanities spills from her, and I can't keep the smirk from my face.

When she sees where we're heading, those profanities turn to pleas.

"No, you wouldn't. Please no."

Too late.

I toss her into the lake without a second thought.

The splash she makes has me chuckling. She's going to be so mad.

She splutters as she breaks the surface, but she needs to be taught a lesson as she seems to listen when Gianna lays them down. I walk into the water, and when she tries to stand, I shove her back down. She peers up at me, surprised.

"Oops, I slipped."

A scream tears from her throat as she frantically fights against the water and the weight of her dress to stand. But the only way to achieve what I need is for her to fear me.

She once trusted me, and look what happened.

No, that won't work.

I hate myself for it, but I remind myself this is all part of the plan to save her, and I guess for that to happen, I have to show her how badly she wants to live.

Forgive me...

Before she has a chance to find her footing, I grip the back of her neck and shove her head into the water, holding her down. She fights frantically, but I don't let her go.

Her hands skim the water, tugging at invisible hands to help her.

But the only person who can help her is herself.

I count to fifteen before lifting her face out of the water, but I don't let her stand.

"You fucker!" she wheezes, slapping her fists against the water. "Let me go!"

I do the opposite and shove her face back down again.

My heart hurts. But a part of me also likes it.

It's the part that makes Valentina and me one and the same.

I understand her because I *am* her.

I too get off on the violence.

I too feel most alive in the blood and chaos.

But I don't want that life for her.

I grapple with my morals every single day, and sometimes, I'm afraid the demons will conquer me because it's so much easier being bad than being good.

I yank her face out of the water, enraged. "Killing a man makes you feel alive? Is that it?"

She struggles madly, the fight in her never dying. And I don't expect anything less. That is why Gianna will use her as her most powerful weapon.

She will destroy the innocent girl who looked at me with terror but curiosity from that attic window. And I'm afraid she will never look at me like that again.

I'm afraid that I will no longer recognize the girl who saved me when she didn't have to—she saved me in so many ways.

She bargained for my freedom like we were a package deal.

No one has ever given a shit about me my entire life, no one but her and Lewis. That is why I need to save them both.

I might be too late for Lewis, but I'm not too late for her.

"You're such a fucking hero," I mock, bending low and getting in her face. "Killing a man and pretending you don't care."

"I don't care!"

"Life means so little to you, does it?"

"Yes, I don't care! I don't care about anything. I don't care about you! I don't care about that fucking man! I don't care about anyone! I don't care because I feel nothing. Feelings do nothing but hurt. And I'm sick of hurting! I've been hurting my entire life!"

"Boo-fucking-hoo!" I scream inches from her face. "Get over it. That excuse doesn't stick. It makes you sound like a whiny little bitch."

Her eyes widen, and she tries to grab me, but I dodge her.

"I hate you!"

"Good."

"You've not spoken to me for years because you're upset I kicked your ass? Who's the whiny little bitch?"

"Oh, please. I have better things to do than waste my time

on some immature little girl."

"I wasn't a little girl when I slit that man's throat," she says with pride.

And that's what I need to flush from her mind.

I need her to feel. Not switch off. I need her to hold on to her humanity before she is lost to me forever.

"It was survival of the fittest. He lost, and I won. I don't care if I live or die. All I care about is getting my revenge!"

That arrogance will get her killed. One day, she will underestimate the wrong person, and they will say the same thing to her as they end her life.

"Let's test that theory out, then."

She opens her mouth, about to curse me out, but I shove her head back down into the water.

I hold her down for ten seconds.

Then let her back up for five before forcing her back under.

I hold her down for fifteen seconds.

Then let her back up for ten and so forth until she is dunked under the water more than out of it.

The fight in her never dies, however. Her spirit is strong, just as I knew it would be.

I count down from ten, and when I reach one, I yank her out.

She gasps for air, her mouth like a fish out of water, and I hope she remembers this if she ever gambles with her life.

"Don't care whether you live or die?" I taunt, finally letting her go. "Think of this moment whenever you fool yourself into thinking that is true."

She doesn't attempt to rise as she catches her breath.

She looks like a drowned cat, but as the full moon comes out of hiding, I've never seen a more beautiful sight.

We will always be joined in one way or another, and I will fight for her safety and her humanity even when she doesn't want me to.

"I hate you," she says once again, but the way she is looking at me, how a girl looks at a boy, we both know that's not true.

But I won't touch her that way.

Not until she asks me. And not until she's a woman who can make choices that are hers alone.

"No, *tesoro mio*, you hate yourself that you don't."

A furious scream has me grinning from ear to ear as I leave her alone to lick her wounds.

CHAPTER 8

LENNY

I watch.

Like I do most nights.

Hoping that he will come.

But like most nights, he never does.

But tonight is different.

Tonight is different because I will make him come to me.

I slink into my hoodie as I adjust it around my face. Now is a time when I don't want to stand out in the crowd. Well, not for my looks anyhow.

This deserted factory once manufactured chocolate. Now,

nothing sweet is made here. This place is so far off the beaten path that the cops don't even bother coming out here anymore. The brave assholes who call this place home are their own authorities and pass judgment how they deem fit, which is why I need to watch my ass.

Here, I am the underdog.

Not the alpha.

But I need to run with this pack.

So I have to play nice.

Roll over.

Sit.

Whatever they say, I have to do.

I don't make eye contact with anyone, but I swear to fuck, the dregs of society call this place their home. It's a cesspool of filth. But I need to use these fuckers to show Aldo that I'm different.

And that's why I'm here.

I've gone back to ignoring Valentina. It's fair to say that her hatred for me has grown. But my plan worked. I see that her focus has changed in the way she trains with Franklin. She doesn't fight in haste. She watches and strategizes.

Gianna has been quiet since the night of the party. I know that's because she is up to something. What, however, I don't know.

Which is why I'm here.

I wanted to prove my loyalty to Aldo another way. But time is running out.

I can't go to Aldo and spill Gianna's secrets because I'll be seen as disloyal. I'll be seen as a rat. And if I could betray the woman who "raised" me, why wouldn't I betray a man I don't know? He will assume Gianna sent me.

I don't need to draw a diagram of how that scenario ends— me without my head.

So I have to be smart.

I need to prove myself. They need to do their homework without me telling them who I am.

And that is why I fall back behind the crowd, watching two meatheads smack the shit out of each other. Men from all wakes of life holler at their favorites, clutching onto their colored ticket stubs like it's their golden ticket.

I laugh at the analogy.

It's our very own Willy Wonka Fight Club.

The men are all brawn, no brains. They are built like brick shithouses, but that doesn't make a good fighter. One man has a blue sash. The other a red. That's the only way the spectators know who's who. No names are used. No friends are made.

This is about making money and, of course, to find minions for Aldo.

Three men stand off to the side. Two are identical twins. The other looks to be about twelve years old. But looks are deceiving because I know they're lethal. They are also Aldo's men, so I need to get them on my side.

The crowd cheers when Blue pushes Red into the circle of rabid men. They shove the half-dead man back into Blue, who punches him square in the jaw. Red wavers before falling flat onto his face.

The fight is done.

Red tickets are crumpled into tight balls and tossed onto the ground in rage as they have bet on the wrong horse. Blue tickets are held tightly, however, because their champion has won.

A man in overalls grips Red by the feet and drags his unconscious body from the circle. No one looks twice.

No one here cares about humanity. Only money.

The open fire drums cackle loudly, illuminating this shithole in oranges and yellows and amplifying the bloodstains on the broken concrete. The structure is barely standing. It sets the perfect scene for a battlefield I'm about to conquer and defeat.

A man with a pink sash soon takes Red's place and charges Blue without warning. The animalistic screams of the men reflect the hard-ons they have for violence. It seems we're all sick fucks, animated by bloodshed and carnage.

Blue reads his move. This isn't his first rodeo, judging by the many scars on his face and body. I dare say he's the crowd favorite, which means I'm going to have fun knocking his ass to the ground.

I study the way he moves.

He's taller and bigger than me. But that isn't going to be an issue. I've fought bigger than him before and won.

He counts to three before he punches. I read it in the way he hesitates before each punch. And on cue, he confirms my suspicions.

One…

Two…

Three…

Punch.

Pink takes the hit and springs back, getting in a shot which seems to shock Blue.

Not only is he a trash fighter but he's arrogant too.

This is really going to be too easy.

With my head bowed, I subtly push my way past the frothing assholes who are focused on nothing but the slabs of meat who are their cash cows. No one pays any attention to me. I don't look like a threat. And this will be their downfall.

I stand off to the side, ensuring I'm not in anyone's way.

Blue is the winner of this fight. Pink doesn't stand a chance. I wonder if perhaps this is rigged because this isn't a fair fight. That would explain why Blue's face looks like he had a late-night rendezvous with a mulcher.

This isn't his first rodeo.

The crowd is wild as the men fight, and when Blue shoves Pink, he stumbles backward, straight into me. Blue comes charging toward him, but Pink sidesteps, and when Blue swings, he connects with my jaw.

The frenzied screams of the men suddenly cease, the echo of their ecstasy the only thing that pulsates in the air. I grin, wiping the trickle of blood from my mouth with my thumb. Before Blue can get out a word, I punch him square in the face.

The heightened energy of the rabid men is almost suffocating because they know what's about to happen. So does Pink as he disappears into the throngs of people since this isn't his fight any longer.

Blue shakes his head, stunned, but soon recovers.

It's on.

We charge for one another, but he doesn't stand a chance because he's my way in. I know Aldo's men are watching, and I plan on making an example out of Blue.

I punch him again, catching him unawares. He staggers back, and I then deliver an uppercut. I hear his teeth crunch, and when he spits one out, it bounces on the ground, and he knows his luck is over.

He looks in the direction of the three men, confirming my suspicions—this fight is rigged.

I hate cheaters.

But to be fair, I do hate most people, and Blue is the person

I plan on taking my anger out on.

I punch him in the ribs, the stomach, and then deliver a combo of punches to his face. I was trained to fight and fight properly, so this dirty rat doesn't stand a chance.

He is heavy on his feet, his meaty fists attempting to connect with me, but I duck to the left, then the right as he swings, and the moment he's open, I king-hit him in the face.

He wavers on his feet, attempting to focus, but I wave him good night as he collapses onto his front, out cold.

The bloodlust rouses my demons, but I keep them at bay. I need Aldo's men to see control and discipline. I need them to see my value so they invite me in.

The silence is soon filled with raucous roars as men slap me on the back. I'm their new victor, but I shrug them off because I didn't do this to make new friends. Slipping my hoodie back on, I make a beeline for the exit, but one of the twins steps forward, blocking my path.

He sizes me up.

I stand unwavering, and when he doesn't move, I chuckle. "Unless you're about to buy me dinner and show me a good time, I suggest you move."

I attempt to push past Tweedledee, but his brother, Tweedledum, steps in.

"Oh, look," I quip, folding my arms across my chest. "There are two of you...your poor mother."

Tweedledum snarls, but the younger-looking dude appears, calming these jacked-up fucks down. He's clearly in charge. The two bigger guys are the beef. And this dude is the brains.

Again, looks can be deceiving because this dude may seem harmless, weak even, but that works in his favor, tricking presumptuous fucks who'll regret underestimating his size.

"What's your name?"

I simply laugh in response.

His poker face doesn't slip, and I know he plays hardball. "You're here for a reason. Follow me, pretty boy."

When I don't move, I feel the unmistakable poke of a gun barrel being pressed into the small of my back.

"Since you asked so nicely," I taunt, following him.

The rowdy crowd looks at one another, confused as they don't know who the winner is. I leave behind a storm of chaos—just the way I like it.

A large black SUV is parked ahead.

The door opens as we walk toward it. But no one gets out. Tweedledum nudges me forward with the gun, and I do something really fucking stupid, which is why it's a great idea—I spin around and punch him in the mouth.

He stumbles on his feet and almost trips, which infuriates him. Just as he is about to pistol-whip me, a man's face appears from the back seat of the SUV.

"Enough, Rocco."

A rumble erupts from me. "Nice to see your name is as lame as you are."

Rocco launches forward, but the man scolds him in Italian. It takes all his willpower to hold back, but in the end, the punishment isn't worth kicking my ass for, so he stands down.

"Good dog," I mutter under my breath.

This really is too easy.

I walk toward the SUV, and the man dressed immaculately in a navy pinstripe suit and crisp white shirt has me guessing this is Aldo.

His short dark hair is graying at the temples. At a guess, I'd say he's early fifties. With his good looks and the power he exudes, I can imagine he is loved but also feared.

"I would ask who you are, but I don't think you'd answer me."

"You'd guess right." I slide into the SUV, whistling as I take in the leather interior.

The car smells like a forest after a storm. I'm assuming it's Aldo's cologne.

Rocco and his brother wait outside while the younger dude joins us inside. He closes the door. The privacy screen between the driver's seat and the back seat rolls up, enclosing us like we're one big happy family.

Aldo looks at me with nothing but curiosity.

I like him already.

He doesn't need to assert his authority with threats or bad manners. He reeks of control and power, like a true leader should.

"Drink?"

I nod.

He pours some scotch into a crystal glass, offering it to me. I accept.

He pours one for himself, and I wait. I'm his guest after all.

"Shall we make a toast?"

I shrug, waiting for him to make a point because I know there is one.

"To prosperity and good health." He raises his glass.

I raise mine.

"Saluti."

"Cheers."

I don't want to give away my Italian roots. I need him to believe our meeting was fate.

We both throw back our drinks.

I wait again because, like Aldo, I wish to exert my power through composure, not fear. He doesn't speak. Simply smiles. But this is a test. You can tell a lot about a person by how they respond to silence.

Someone who can sit alone in a setting filled with noise and be utterly content in their own company is totally comfortable within themselves. They don't need friends to entertain them because they enjoy their own company best.

I know this feeling well because I'm not a people person.

I would much rather be comfortable in the silence than fill it with bullshit small talk. It's not something that a lot of people can do, and that's because most people would rather engage in nonsense than face the reality that is their lives.

But men like Aldo, they are always alone.

They may come across as a social being, but it's all for looks.

People are a means to an end. We all serve a purpose in someone's story. If they think we will benefit them somehow, they offer us their time and energy because everyone wants something from someone.

We're all in it for ourselves. Anyone who says otherwise is lying.

And when our purpose is fulfilled, then it's thanks for the memories.

NEXT!

We live in a disposable world; sad but true.

But men like Aldo flourish in the silence, and when they find a fellow lone wolf, he sees in them what he does in himself, which is strength.

Although they work alone, they need an army of like-minded men who see that he too serves a purpose in *their* story and will do what they must to get what they want.

Never think anyone is doing anything out of the kindness

of their heart.

Rookie mistake number one.

However, this is Aldo's territory, so I show him the respect he expects.

"You fight with skill." He crosses an ankle over his knee. "I won't waste either of our time by asking who taught you."

I nod, appreciating him not boring us with small talk.

"You're here with purpose, so what is it? Please don't insult me and deny it. Tell me what it is you want."

I match his composure. "It's only a matter of time until someone wants more because someone *always* wants more."

Aldo listens intently.

"That dumbass you have fighting for you? He's cocky, which makes him stupid. He thinks he's untouchable, which also makes him dangerous."

"Why is this your concern?" the guy whose name I still don't know asks.

"Because I'm confident, not cocky. I know to never underestimate the underdog." I make a point to look at him because I saw through him the moment I laid eyes on him. "I'm also a better fighter. I'm a better fighter than most."

"And what good is that to us?" he questions while Aldo listens.

"I don't want any enemies. I'm not interested in overthrowing your empire. I only want what is owed to me because of the work I put in. Let me fight for you, and you won't need to rig any matches because I'll win fair and square.

"At the moment, I assume you organize the fights to take place in these shitholes because you want to keep it low-key. But if I fight for you, we aim for bigger and better. And that means more bodies, more money…and more motherfuckers to sell your gear to."

The guy reaches behind him to no doubt pull a piece on me, but Aldo shakes his head once.

"You're a very clever young man. You got all this from watching?"

I nod.

Aldo mulls over my comment before brushing invisible dirt from his vest. I notice a gold pinkie ring with a purple stone. "If this young man was able to see all this, you failed at your job, Glenn."

A laugh escapes me because his name is *Glenn*? For real?

Glenn knows better than to challenge his boss.

"What is owed to you?" Aldo asks, circling back to what I said.

"I win fights and do whatever jobs you need me to do. I give you my loyalty, and in return, I find my brother."

Glenn scoffs, but something changes in Aldo, and I wonder if that something has to do with Valentina.

"Family is invaluable," he says with sincerity. "A man may

have many riches, but without family, he is penniless."

He speaks from experience.

"What do you know of crystals?"

"Crystals?" I ask in case I misheard him.

But it's apparent I haven't when he nods. "Different crystals have their own energies which can align one's life in all different ways."

I wait for the punchline, but there is none.

"Have you worked behind a counter?"

I shake my head, unsure if this is code for something.

He reaches into the console and produces a business card.

I accept and silently read over the description.

Aldo Cattaneo—Opal imports and lapidary.

I was right about one thing at least. But crystals, really?

I can't really imagine Aldo sitting under a full moon in a drum circle while summoning the goddess of health to grant him inner peace.

This has to be a front, and a smart one at that.

"Come to that address tomorrow. Ten a.m. If you're interested."

And just like that, I'm dismissed.

I pocket the business card and open the door, but Aldo has one last thing to say before I go.

"Be careful what you're willing to sacrifice because sometimes the past is best left alone. I'm Aldo, by the way."

"Lennon," I finally reveal.

It's not a warning but free advice, which I assume he doesn't give out often. I don't know how I know, but I just do—Aldo and I are going to be great friends.

It's late by the time I arrive home.

The urge to check in on Valentina, as always, has me heading into the kitchen instead. Opening the fridge, I grab a beer. Tossing the cap into the sink, I throw it back and ponder over tonight's fucked-up proceedings.

I'm not naive. I know Aldo will test me before he welcomes me into the "family." I wonder what I'll have to give up to achieve what I want.

The thought has me downing the rest of the beer.

"You're home late."

Gianna making small talk?

This won't end well.

"Couldn't sleep," I reply bluntly, throwing the empty beer bottle into the trash. "Night."

I attempt to walk past her, but she grips my wrist.

I exhale slowly because I don't like being touched, and she knows this. She usually respects my space, but as I look at her, I know the plan I thought she was formulating is about to be put into play.

"You smell"—she searches for the right words but settles for something I'm certain she didn't intend—"different."

"I went for a run. I'm about to hit the shower."

It's a blunt hint, one she ignores.

"What happened to your face?"

"I ran into a door."

Her lips twist into a smirk, but it's akin to a spider as she watches her prey, trapped in her web, attempting to set itself free.

"I've taught you better than that. Sarcasm is a fool's tool. If you have something to say, then say it."

I snatch my arm back and glare at her. I only just realize that she's wearing a sheer nightgown, and the moonlight shining into the large windows accentuates her bare form beneath.

The analogy of the spider suddenly is more accurate than I thought.

"I want to know where my brother is," I say blankly, tired of her games. "I also want to know what exactly you want with Valentina."

"I want the best for her. I want the best for you both."

I scoff, unmoved by her lies.

"And the best for her is killing a man?"

Gianna brushes back her long hair.

She is beautiful. A femme fatale with her long black hair

and red lips. I hate to admit it, but it's the truth. But her ugliness on the inside overshadows any exterior beauty.

"I didn't raise little crybabies. But perhaps I underestimated you."

She's baiting me, so I remain calm.

"You're an adult now, Lenny. You can leave at any time. But you choose to stay. We both know why that is."

There is a double meaning to her words.

I stay for Lewis.

But more so, I stay for Valentina.

"I do not know where your brother is."

"Bullshit. You're nothing but a fucking liar."

She appears taken aback that I've spoken to her this way. I brace for her wrath, but what I get has me wondering if I'm fucking dreaming.

She steps forward and begins rubbing over the front of my jeans.

I slap her hand away, disgusted and horrified. "What the *fuck* are you doing?"

But she's not deterred and grips my cock.

"Seeing as you finally found your balls—"

"Knock it off."

This seductress shit won't fly with me because she can try every trick in the book, but I would rather cut off my dick than succumb to her ways.

"We all have wants in this world that need to be fulfilled. You fulfill mine. I fulfill yours."

She just confirmed what I always knew to be true. She knows where Lewis is, and it seems the only way to make her talk is to fuck her.

What a predicament I find myself in.

I stand feet above her, but her small stature doesn't fool me like it would most. I've seen this woman take down men three times her size. But I now see her greatest weapon is the air of seduction she carries to make men grovel on their knees.

So I decide to do the complete opposite.

The way her nipples press against the thin material of her nightgown and the throbbing at the side of her throat are all dead giveaways that she's affected by me, which I plan on exploiting for my own gain—something she taught me.

I stop fighting and allow her to rub over my cock, wanting her to see that she can go to town all she wants, but I'm going to be softer than Justin Bieber.

"Sorry, sweetheart, you're just not doing it for me."

She appears genuinely upset as I assume no man has ever said such a thing to her. But no man has ever despised her more than me.

But this is something I can use because sex is power, which is what she just tried to prove. She just didn't think it would backfire. But it's worked in my favor because she taught me that every predator disguises himself to lure in his prey.

She really shouldn't have underestimated me.

She opens her mouth, but I spin her around, trapping her against the counter as I press my chest into her back. She smells like flowers. I want to puke from the sickly sweet scent.

"I know what you're doing," I say into her ear.

She tries to buck me off, but we both know if she wanted to get free, she could.

She likes this.

"And I'm surprised. Is this why you *adopted* me?" I don't hold back on the sarcasm because never once have we been one big happy family.

I have never seen her as a mother figure.

Nor have I seen Valentina as my sister.

We are not a family in that sense.

Which is why I have no qualms lifting the hem of Gianna's nightgown and exposing her bare ass. It's a great ass; too bad it belongs to the she-devil in heels.

I smack her ass—hard. So hard that she propels up the counter from the force.

She splays her hands on the marble, but it's no use when I smack her again.

"Is this what you want? Actually, you know, don't answer that because I don't give a fuck what you want."

I smack her ass one last time before spinning her back

around. Her eyes are wide. Lips parted. Her breaths fast.

I look at her with nothing but loathing.

She awaits further command, which, again, surprises me. She exerts nothing but control, but in the bedroom, is she a sub?

I guess there's only one way I'll ever know.

I don't ask.

I take.

Yanking up her nightgown, I let it be known that I'll do with her as I please as I order, "Get yourself off because I sure as fuck am not going to."

When she hesitates, I spit on her pussy. "That's the only help you'll be getting from me."

A low moan escapes her, and she does as I say and begins fingering herself. Our eyes are locked the entire time. She bites her lip and spreads her legs wider.

I would be lying if I didn't admit this turned me on a little. But not in the traditional sense. The power I have over her is what's getting me off.

Perhaps I've found something I can control her with. I will *never* fuck her. But fuck *with* her?

Hell to the fuck yes.

She sinks two fingers into her pussy, pleasuring herself leisurely. Her pussy is like a Venus flytrap—trapping her unsuspecting prey to fulfill her carnivorous needs.

I laugh at the analogy, which enrages her.

"Should we call Valentina down here to watch? Perhaps she could learn a thing or two."

The moment she says her name, I launch forward and grab her by the throat, squeezing hard.

A winded laugh escapes her.

"Do not speak her name."

"Have I not taught you nothing? You continue to lead with your emotions. And that girl, she'll be the death of you…in every single way."

"What do you know of emotions, you heartless bitch?"

I tighten my grip and arch her neck backward, seething inches from her face.

The violence turns her on. I can hear by her breathless whimpers as well as how wet she is.

"I would rather lead with something other than greed because your empire won't stand forever. It will crumble before your eyes. I'll make sure of it."

This isn't helping me in any way, but I am done. She'll never tell me where Lewis is. I've given up on that notion. But I can't abandon Valentina.

"And that is why I have made mine yours, you silly, silly boy. Would you really destroy your own legacy? Would you destroy *hers*?" She gasps before climaxing with a sated moan as she reads the horror on my face.

I stand speechless because fuck me, I thought I was playing her, but…she fucking played me.

She smears her arousal across my lips with a victorious grin.

I wipe it away with disgust.

"One hundred and eleven Broadway Avenue…that's where you'll find the answers you seek."

She pushes past me, freshly fucked.

While me…I'm just fucked.

CHAPTER 9

LENNY

The reason I've not set this crack house on fire is because Lewis may be inside. But the thought of him being inside here is just too hard to fathom.

My mom was a junkie. There's no way Lewis would touch that shit. But could it be the case of the apple doesn't fall far from the tree?

I don't even want to think about that right now.

First and foremost, I need to watch and learn because acting on impulse will not work in my favor.

If Lewis is in here, then it's because he wants to be, hooked on whatever shit he's putting into his body, and I know a happy family reunion isn't in the cards for us.

I failed him when I promised that I would protect him.

He has every right to hate me.

Knowing he may have followed in the footsteps of our mom has me gripping the pendant around my throat, wishing for direction more than ever.

I have to meet Aldo soon, but I couldn't not come here first.

I needed to see if what Gianna said held any weight. So far, I'm hoping she's full of shit because if Lewis is here, then I fear he's lost to me forever.

But that doesn't mean I won't try.

I'll try until the day I die to save him. But I fear he may get there first.

A young woman with pink hair comes out of the front door. She's wearing a school uniform. I watch with interest. She looks from left to right before taking the three stairs and hitting the pavement.

I want to ask her if she's seen Lewis. But I don't even know what he looks like. Or if he's changed his name.

Did he grow tall? Strong? Is he still as stubborn as always?

I hate that I don't know the answers to these questions.

And besides, I can't ask anyone just yet because word will get back to him, and he'll run. And then I'm back to square one.

I finally have a lead.

So I can't blow it.

But patience isn't my strong suit.

I decide to follow her, though.

I keep a fair distance behind and ensure I remain as inconspicuous as possible. She's tapping her fingers on her leg to whatever song is playing in her earbuds. Rookie move. She walks about without her hearing, a vital sense we need to ensure no one is following us, like right now.

She crosses the street in no real hurry, which makes me believe she isn't strung out. She doesn't appear to be jonesing for her next fix, which has me thinking she's a dealer.

So the question is, where does she get the gear from?

I follow until she reaches an upmarket apartment complex, a completely different vibe from the crack house she was just in.

Now, this is something I was not expecting.

I have all the answers I'm going to get today, so I cross the street and make my way to Aldo's store. It's in a rough part of town. I'm not sure the demographic here would have any use for crystals, well, not the kind Aldo sells anyway.

I was half expecting this to be a joke, but when I see the storefront, I'm glad I'm not a betting man.

Pure Opalence.

That's what Aldo's store is called, a clever play on words for so many reasons.

The bell above the door alerts my arrival. I'm instantly hit with sandalwood and soft, calming music the moment I enter. The place is small but stocked well. Crystal ornaments, crystal jewelry, and all crystals known to humankind are laid out strategically.

A sign near the counter with an arrow pointing at the red curtain lets customers know you can get your palm or tarot read for ten bucks.

If I wasn't standing here in chakra alley, then I would never believe my eyes.

I walk over to the huge crystal rock in the corner of the room. I have no idea what it does, but priced at fifteen thousand dollars, I would hope it could bring world peace.

"That's an amethyst. The all-purpose stone," says a voice I recognize as Aldo from behind me.

"For that price tag, I would hope its purpose would include cleaning my house and doing my laundry for the rest of my life."

Turning around, I meet a smiling Aldo. He's dressed in black pants and a white shirt. He's all business, looking very professional in a place where Crocs and tie-dye shirts are usually the norm.

He reads my thoughts. "You don't believe in this"—he searches for the right word—"mumbo jumbo?"

I laugh because if anyone else were to use that term, I would punch them in the face. "I guess I'm more of a practical man. I believe in anything that proves itself to me. If your crystals here can offer anything other than pretty colors, then sure, sign me up."

Aldo mulls over my comment before bursting into laughter. *"Mi piaci."*

I nod, pretending I have no idea Aldo just said he likes me.

"I have to go out for an hour. Think you can handle the place while I'm gone?"

Another test.

"As long as I don't need to read anyone's palm, I'm sure I can figure it out."

"There's freshly brewed herbal tea out back."

"To do what with?"

"To drink," Aldo replies, still laughing.

"And it'll still be there when you get back."

Herbal fucking tea.

Aldo leaves, trusting me with his merchandise because he knows I wouldn't steal a thing in this store. What the fuck am I supposed to do with a soleus balancing charm?

I go behind the counter and see an old-fashioned till. Pushing a few buttons on it, I get the hang of it soon enough, but I doubt I'll be making any sales. Because who the fuck would buy anything from here?

Poking my head through the red curtain, I can't contain my chuckle when I see the small circular table covered by a black velvet tablecloth with a crystal ball atop it.

There's got to be a catch.

I don't even bother looking into the small kitchenette 'cause the herbal tea was enough of a hint that I won't like anything in there.

The bell sounds, alerting me that someone just entered. I expect to see Aldo, revealing he was just joking about leaving me unsupervised, but it's a woman in yoga gear carrying a tote with a picture of a cow and the slogan "Don't have a cow, man" written across it.

She has in her earbuds so she doesn't hear me when I emerge from the back. I stand behind the counter, watching her to see if perhaps she's here for another reason besides the decor. She reaches for some wind chimes, which make a god-awful ruckus.

How the fuck does one find harmony in what sounds like a four-year-old bashing two glass bottles together while listening to Metallica?

"Do you have this but with tiger's eye?" she asks, holding up some circular ornament.

When I look at her like she just spoke in Swahili, she removes an earbud. Perhaps she thinks I didn't hear her, but I heard her loud and clear. I just don't understand the question.

"I thought you'd be against animal cruelty." When it's her turn to look at me like I've just spoken in another language, I jut my chin out toward her bag.

She peers down at it, as if forgetting what bag she has. After a second, she giggles. "Not literal tiger's eye. The stone, I mean."

"Oh, my bad. Honestly, you'd have more idea than I would," I reply blankly. "I only know that thing is an atheist or something."

"Amethyst," she corrects with a small smile.

"Yeah, right. See? Point proven."

I leave her to her shopping because right now, I sound like a dumbass. I open the drawers behind the counter in hopes of finding something that will prove my hunch that this place is just a sham to conceal the illegal dealings that really take place here.

But I find nothing as expected.

"I'll take these."

I forgot the woman was here because that's how interesting her tiger's eye talk was. She smiles when I look at the array of goods she places on the counter.

Some are household items with crystals in them. I honestly don't know about the other stuff and won't embarrass myself further by trying to guess.

I ring up the total and blanch when this pile of junk comes in at over a hundred bucks. But the woman looks at me, confused.

When she reads my puzzlement, she clarifies, "Oh, Aldo said he left a bag of quartz for me?"

Her comment piques my interest because this is surely code for drugs.

I fucking knew it.

"My name is Chanty. He said it was in the back," she adds before I can ask.

"Be right back."

I round the corner and see a door down the end of the skinny hallway. I have no idea what I'm about to find when I open it. I peer around the doorjamb, expecting to see it stocked high with drugs, guns, and everything else illegal, but when I see crystals and stones, I don't know whether to be disappointed or relieved.

This isn't going how I thought.

Remembering I have a customer, I quickly check the shelves for her order and am definitely disappointed when I see a bag of white and pink stones with her name on it.

"What the fuck am I missing here?" I mumble under my breath as I grab the bag and make my way back into the store.

When she sees her goods, she smiles happily.

I add the bag of crap to the total, which comes to over five hundred dollars. "What are you doing with this shit?" I ask, genuinely curious.

She stops rifling through her bag. Her eyes widen before she composes herself. "I teach art."

She offers no other explanation.

She pays me in cash and places her items in her tote. I assume she's a "say no to plastics" kinda girl.

"Thanks. I'll see you next week."

I don't ask why the fuck she needs more rock 'cause what kind of art class does she teach? I am so out of my element right now.

Chanty leaves while I wonder what I've missed. There's nothing here to prove my suspicions. Everything has a place. It's clean—too clean.

Something is amiss.

But what?

The bell once again chimes, hinting yet another customer is here.

Am I wrong? Could Aldo really be an upstanding citizen who runs a legitimate business selling…crystals?

I snort out a laugh because what in the ever-living mumbo jumbo is happening?

"Who are you?"

Could it be that being among all this spiritual shit has awoken my third eye? Is the universe talking to me like a book I saw on the shelf said it does?

Whatever the reason, I'm going to take it as a sign because who stands before me is the girl with the pink hair.

I look at her.

She looks at me.

When I don't say a word, she folds her arms across her chest. "Are you another exchange student my dad sponsored without telling me?"

She assumes I don't understand her because I'm looking at her with a deer-in-the-headlights look. But there is no fucking way she is who I think she is 'cause if she is, then I *was* right. And nothing gets me harder than being right.

"I'm Lenny. Aldo asked me to watch the store for him. He'll be back in an hour."

She doesn't make it a secret she's examining me closely. She doesn't trust me. Nor does she like me. "This is so typical of Aldo."

She makes a beeline for the back, but I quickly sidestep, blocking her path.

She does not appreciate me doing this. I'm twice her size, but she doesn't let that intimidate her. Her long hair is the color of cotton candy. And her eyes are green. She's beautiful, but I don't mistake her beauty for softness. She is all attitude, which is my favorite kind.

"Oh my God, you're even lamer than Rocco, and that's saying something. Move, pretty boy." She shoves me out of the way, heading into the kitchen while my brain finally plays catch-up.

"Aldo is your father." It's not a question but rather a statement.

She pauses from sipping her tea, looking at me over the rim of her mug like I am a daft little bitch. "The more you speak, the more I want to punch you in the face."

She finishes her tea before hunting through the drawer and placing a bag of green stones into her schoolbag. "I'm late, and you're wasting my time. Let's never do this again."

She doesn't give me a chance to get a word in edgewise and, once again, shoves me out of the way, leaving the store without another word.

What the fuck just happened?

I'm even more confused than ever, but what I do know is that Aldo's daughter may know where Lewis is. If this is a sign from the universe, then I am now a fucking believer.

Aldo returns an hour later, offering to pay me, which I, of course, decline.

I don't mention his daughter because, again, I don't want to arouse any suspicion. So when he asks me to meet him tomorrow same time, same place, I agree without question.

Gianna asked me to pick up a new car from a dealership, which is not uncommon for her. Then she sent me a list that made me wonder if I was shopping for a frat party.

So when I drive the Mercedes convertible into the garage

and hear Limp Bizkit, I'm prepared to walk into just that.

With groceries in hand, I walk around the back, and what I see has me almost tripping over my own damn feet.

Perhaps I'm high from all the incense and crystals and shit, but life isn't that kind because Valentina *is* really in the pool with two fuckhead jocks while Gianna lounges on a chair, reading a book.

What the fuck alternative universe is this?

"Oh, look, the errand boy is back with the snacks," Valentina says, treading water. "I hope you got cherry cola."

She peers at the six-pack of beer I'm holding while I stand speechless. What in the ever-living fuck is going on right now?

Gianna's huge sunglasses take up half her face, but they don't hide her smirk—that fucking bitch.

This is payback for what happened last night.

She knew how fucking angry this would make me because right now, I'm fucking fuming.

One of the guys swims over to the edge of the pool and offers me his fist like we're bros. I look down at the limb, then back up at the fucker. I have on sunglasses, but he reads loud and clear that he has three seconds to get the fuck out of my face before I use my own fist to punch out his teeth.

He swims away to safety.

Apart from the obvious, something is very wrong with Valentina. She is pissed off—more so than usual, that is.

I don't know what happened last night for her to…

Oh fuck.

Did she see what happened between Gianna and me? Or perhaps Gianna told her? This would explain the insanity I'm currently witnessing.

And when Valentina stands, revealing the skimpy red bikini she's wearing, as if making a point, it seems my inkling may be true.

God, her body is fucking perfection. She's curvy and strong. I know how she smells because I want to fucking devour her every time she walks past me. She brushes the wet hair from her face and licks away a droplet of water lingering on her top lip.

I've tried not to think of her this way because nothing good ever comes of it, but goddamn, I'm weak when she's looking at me all wet and sun-kissed. I want to rob her of air as I kiss the fuck out of her while she's pulling my hair. I want to choke the smile from her face until she moans my name.

My cock is about to punch a hole through my jeans.

One of the guys makes it very clear he is eyeing Valentina's breasts. I barely resist the urge to throw a beer can at his stupid face.

She's doing this to get a rise out of me, but I'll be damned if I cave.

I stare her down, making it very clear that she can flaunt her shit all she wants. It doesn't make a difference because I'm not jealous—even though I want to rip off those two motherfuckers' heads and shit down their headless necks.

Gianna waits for me to react. And I do occasionally put her teachings into practice.

I count to three and channel some fucking crystal energy juju, dumping the bags and beer by the pool's edge.

I don't say a word as I turn around and make my way into the house so I can kick the shit out of the punching bag in the gym because I am not jealous—said no one ever.

Namaste, motherfuckers.

CHAPTER 10

VALENTINA

He doesn't care.

And it hurts.

I can pretend that it doesn't.

But it does.

All Lenny ever does is hurt me.

Yet I can't stay away.

But last night, when I saw him and Gianna, that hurt turned to something else.

I wanted to hurt him how he hurt me.

I wanted him to want me how he does Gianna.

But all I've done is make a fool of myself.

These two guys, whose names I've already forgotten, were here tending to the gardens when Gianna invited them to join us in the pool. I was surprised she even offered, but when she suggested we ask Lenny to bring back some snacks, I jumped at the chance, hoping to make him jealous.

I wondered if she too was hoping to achieve this because, knowing Lenny, he probably hasn't spoken two words to her after spitting on her pussy and watching her play with herself for him.

I am angry and disgusted at both of them because I feel like the third wheel.

Gianna can have any man she wants, so why Lenny?

Something competitive and primeval has come over me because Lenny is mine. I don't recognize this emotion because it's one I wasn't taught, but I don't think this can be learned.

I don't know if I want to scream or cry.

All I know is that the ache between my legs won't go away. And it only seems to grow when I think about Lenny and Gianna since I wish it were me.

The guys bored me after twenty minutes, but I stayed in hopes that maybe I could find those butterflies girls my age do with boys their age.

But I didn't find anything other than wondering who would scream the loudest if I kneed them in the balls.

Gianna left with the younger out of the two, leaving me alone with Ashton.

Or was it Adam?

I don't even know or care because when he tried to kiss me, I acted on instinct and punched him in the face.

He left after he nursed his bleeding lip and bruised ego.

So I did the only thing that I've read about and makes sense—I drank the beers Lenny bought and am now a little drunk.

Well, I think I am.

It's well past midnight, and I'm sprawled out on the lounge bed, peering up into the skies and tracing the constellations with my finger.

Gianna has taught me how to be book smart, but I'm still the same naive little girl I was when I arrived here all those years ago about life.

Why would she do that?

I thought I didn't care, but now, I think I do.

I think I care that I'm not like everyone else. I care that I'm obsessing over a boy who is a complete and utter asshole when I had Ashton/Adam, who was more than interested.

But he gave me the ick just by…breathing.

Groaning, I gently thump my fist to my forehead in hopes of knocking some sense into me.

Deciding to shower and go to bed, I make my way inside.

No lights are on, but I know this place like the back of my hand.

Or so I thought.

I bump into a wall, which wasn't there before, I swear it wasn't, and that's because the wall is actually a hard chest; Lenny's chest because I know that scent even tipsy it seems.

"Lurking in the shadows like the creep that you are?" I say, my eyes taking a few seconds to focus in the darkness.

He doesn't reply, which infuriates me even further, if that's possible.

"I hate you so fucking much." I know the consequences of my actions, so I reach out with the intent to slap his cheek.

But he's quicker than I am.

He's also sober.

I don't stand a chance.

He doesn't speak.

He doesn't need to.

The anger radiating from every inch of his glorious body burns me and ignites the desire between my legs to an unbearable degree.

I attempt to slap his other cheek, but he snares the other wrist.

I'm now held prisoner by him, but am I really a prisoner when I come willingly?

He's breathless.

So am I.

He's in control, and for once, I like it.

There is a second of clarity before he yanks my arms behind my back, holding my wrists captive in his hand. The other is free, and he uses it to pull my hair, forcing my head back.

It hurts, but it hurts so good.

I can't help myself as I rub my legs together because I'm suddenly so wet.

"I thought you were different."

"I don't care what you thought. Let me go." I try to break free, but he walks us backward, slamming me against the hallway wall.

"We both know you don't mean that."

"Oh, I do mean it, though. I'm *so* tired. Ashton really knows how to show a girl a good time. Perhaps he can give you some pointers."

An animalistic growl slips past Lenny's lips, and my God, nothing has sounded hotter.

"Say his name again. I dare you."

"Ash—"

I don't get a chance to finish my sentence, or breathe, for that matter, because who needs air when Lenny's mouth is on mine?

We freeze, both knowing if we cross this line, there'll be no return…but we don't care.

Lenny forces my mouth open with his, and when I

surrender, he slips in his tongue, seeking out mine. I match his ferocity even though I've never kissed this way before, but I'm a quick learner with Lenny as my teacher.

He bites my lip, and when I gasp, he sucks over the sting before sweeping it over with his tongue.

He isn't gentle. But I don't want gentle.

He dominates my mouth with his—licking, sucking, and biting. I never knew a kiss could feel this way.

I bite his lip hard, so hard I taste blood, and the taste does something to us.

Lenny grabs my throat, choking me as he kisses me with ferocity. I can't keep up with his passion, so I surrender because the way he fucks me with his tongue has me desperate for him to do the same with his fingers.

Lenny is pressed to me, so I can feel he's hard. It doesn't scare me like I thought it would.

What happened in my past, I'll never forget, but it's shaped me into the person I am. No child should ever have to endure what I did.

I was abused.

Molested.

Raped.

I was forced to do and watch horrible things.

But with Lenny, I feel those things don't have to rule me. I can replace the hatred with…love? Or something like it.

I just don't know how to ask for what I want for fear of rejection. And I'm also afraid.

I rub my breasts against his bare chest in hopes he can read my body language. I can't move because my arms are still pinned behind my back, but I mold my body to his, needing more before I explode.

Lenny doesn't speak when he releases my arms. But he's giving me the option to show him what I want, and what I want right now is to feel him inside me.

I place his hand over the front of my bikini bottoms with our lips still locked.

"Are you sure?" he asks, and his kindness touches me.

No man has ever asked permission before, and that is why I place my hand over his, coaxing him to be a memory I want to remember always.

He never ceases kissing me as he glides two fingers up and down the front of my bottoms. Even that feels incredible. I can't imagine what feeling him skin to skin would be like.

I open my legs wider, a silent invitation that I'm okay with more. That I need more.

Thankfully, he doesn't make me beg.

He slows down the kiss, it's languid and hot, and when I relax into the way his tongue strokes mine, he walks his fingers into my bottoms and runs them along my sex. A hiss leaves him when he feels how wet I am.

He continues this for a while, and I find myself getting wetter and wetter. I'm so turned on, and he hasn't even done anything yet. But I'm also impatient.

He chuckles, reading my annoyance.

With one finger, he circles the top of my pussy, and I shudder, and on my exhale, he sinks that finger into me.

A moan escapes me because it feels so good. But that pales compared to when he commences fucking me with that finger.

He kisses from my mouth to my cheek and down to my neck, which he commences kissing as he fingers me.

All I can do is yield because I want this so much. But I know Lenny is an alpha in every sense of the word and wants a submissive girl he can please.

He bites my neck, sucking and licking away the sting. His other hand is on my hip, steadying me because he wants me to relish the feel of him all over me.

When he inserts another finger, my eyes roll to the back of my head because he picks up the speed and is far from gentle. I buck my hips, riding his fingers as he bites my neck.

"Fuck," he says against my neck, his breath hot.

I take that as a cue as him enjoying this as much as me, so I place my hand over his, and we finger fuck me together.

Even in the dark, I can make out those hypnotic eyes, watching me closely, just how he always does. Suddenly, an epiphany hits; I love Lenny, but I also hate him in the same breath. I want to strangle him, but I also want to kiss him until we can no longer breathe.

I don't know if this is what love should feel like, but I do know that I don't want to be without him.

He is the only light in my perpetual darkness. And I fear without him, the darkness will forever eclipse the light, and I will be alone in the shadows for the rest of my days.

"I want—" But I can't say it because I'm mortified I sound so needy.

"What do you want, *tesoro mio*?"

That phrase, I've never understood. It means my love. I always thought he was being sarcastic, but spoken this way, I now see it was always spoken with love.

Not many things in life scare me, but matters of the heart do.

Thankfully, Lenny understands me better than I do myself and takes control. He unties the strap of my bikini behind my neck, pulling down my top and exposing my breasts. He doesn't wait for permission because I'm his…and he knows it.

He takes a breast into his mouth and sucks and licks.

I.

Die.

He's still fingering me as he circles my nipple with his tongue before cupping my breast and doing things with his mouth that have my body trembling, about ready to explode.

Everything is heightened.

I can't control a thing…and the submission, there is a freedom in it. There is liberation in letting go.

Lenny kisses from breast to breast before planting kisses down the middle of my chest. He removes his fingers as those kisses lead farther down.

Over my stomach.

My hips.

Before he circles my belly button with his tongue.

He is soon on his knees before me, peering up, now the one to surrender to me.

The moonlight from the kitchen window is the only light we have, but in the glimmer, it's easier to hide.

He places his fingers into the waistband of my bottoms and slowly takes them off.

I'm standing naked in front of the boy I've loved since I was a child, and nothing has ever felt more right.

However, I stand corrected when he places a single kiss over my sex.

His stubble is coarse, but the sting intensifies my craving, a craving I need fulfilled right now before I explode.

He begins kissing my sex like he did my mouth, slipping his tongue in and out and sucking and licking. On instinct, I grip his hair and use it as reins to move him where I need him to be. He goes willingly, appearing to like it when I take control.

As he is fucking me with his tongue, he slips in a finger and fucks me with both. I've never felt so full.

I want to let go, but a part of me is afraid, and I know that has to do with my past.

Feelings of shame suddenly overcome me as they once did because my innocence was robbed and replaced with depravity, which forever taints something that should be paved with feelings of joy.

I try to block it out, refusing to allow those men to ruin me any more than they already have.

I grind on his face, my bashfulness long gone, but I can't find my release.

I pull on his hair, shoving his face deeper and deeper between my legs, and I can feel the tears approaching.

My high soon fades because all I can hear is that fucking nursery rhyme.

Ring around the rosie…

Anger triumphs and eats my happiness whole.

Am I to be forever broken?

I attempt to push him away, but something happens, something happens to my heart…

"Siamo solo noi. Sempre e solo noi."

Lenny's words of comfort, of him telling me it's only us, it'll only ever just be us, has the wrath subsiding and giving way to a warmth I want to embrace forever.

"*Tu ed io...siamo destinati. Sei mio.* Say it," he orders, demanding I tell him who I belong to.

He sucks over my clit, making my knees buckle because I've never felt this before.

"Say it," he repeats, and when I hesitate, he slaps my ass.

The pain is incredible and echoes where he hit, which has the sadness ebbing away.

"*Io...sonno tua,*" I gasp as he begins eating me out with intensity. "*E tu sei mio.*"

I'm his, but he needs to know that he is also mine.

My words evoke a feral possession, and Lenny is everywhere—hands and mouth, he doesn't give my body a reprieve. He pushes me to the point of everything constricting and clenching in pain because I need to explode.

He circles his tongue inside me so deeply, I feel as though he has taken my breath away from me. I ride his face. I yank his hair. I run my fingernails down his back, relishing the feel of his warm skin and hardened muscles.

He licks my entrance up and down. Side to side. He draws the alphabet with his tongue while I ride it out, feeling my climax approaching.

He uses two fingers to spread me wide and fucks me with his tongue and face, ensuring no part of me is unloved.

It's a heady combination of pleasure and pain.

There is a tenderness to his passion. I want to eat him whole.

Holding him prisoner against my sex, I close my eyes and push out everything but this moment with Lenny. I fuck his face as he fucks me with his tongue. I lose myself to the way he holds my waist, encouraging me to take from him like his mere purpose is to please me.

And please me, he does.

He does something with his tongue, and when he hooks one leg over his shoulder, opening me wider to his touch, I cry out in utter ecstasy, coming hard.

My entire body is rocked from the inside out, and I'm unsure when it'll end. The bad memories are pushed aside and no longer at the forefront because, for the first time in my life, this experience is one I wanted.

I never thought I could enjoy being this way with another, but I'm not afraid.

I feel safe.

He never lets me go.

He never stops.

He allows me to chase my release, ensuring this is a memory I will want to remember for the rest of my life.

And I will.

My heart is beating so fast, I'm afraid it's about to burst from my chest. But the thrill reminds me of the excitement I felt when I ended that asshole's life. Perhaps sex and violence do go hand in hand. Is that what I need to feel something other than nothing at all?

Only when my body stops trembling does Lenny stand, and he does something that touches me so—he presses his forehead to mine, and we bask in this incredible closeness that only we understand.

But I soon realize I'm a selfish lover because Lenny has needs too.

I reach down, finding him to be exceptionally hard against his jeans. I rub over his erection, but he surprises me when he attempts to shift away.

Am I doing something wrong?

I guess he's had more experienced girls giving him a hand job. The thought of another girl's hands on him has me wishing to replace anyone who dared touch what is mine.

"This was for you," he clarifies, as if reading my insecurities.

"What about you?"

"Trust me, that *was* for me as much as it was for you."

"I highly doubt that."

When he reaches down to stop me, I flick open the button of his jeans and reach inside. I'm not surprised to find that he isn't wearing any boxers.

A heavy exhale leaves him as I rub over his thick, hard cock. I don't know what I'm doing. My strokes also feel untrained, attempting to maneuver around something so big. But I think I'm doing okay as a string of profanity spills from Lenny's lips.

But his jeans are in the way. I want them off.

Lenny is now the one to surrender to me, and the hunted is soon to become the hunter. I remove my hand from his jeans and spin him, slamming his back against the wall.

I want to eat him alive.

I start at his neck and bite over his throbbing pulse. A groan passes his delicious lips. It's all the encouragement I need.

I kiss my way down to his collarbones, then I lick a path to each across his broad chest. I can smell the sunshine on his skin.

I lick down the middle of his chest, and when I reach his abs, I find myself getting turned on again. Dropping to my knees, I trace each ridge with my tongue, which elicits a moan from Lenny. I use my fingers to scratch down his stomach. When I get to his V-muscle, I bite over it, sucking away the sting.

He threads his large fingers through my hair, using it as reins, directing me where he wants me. He never lets go of his dominance, which I love.

His cock is huge, and I'm worried I won't be able to please him as he did me.

But I have to at least try.

With my hands pressed to his stomach for balance, I take his dick into my mouth and begin to suck.

"*Oh, cazzo!*"

His cursing spurs me on.

I take as much as I can of him, but soon, he hits the back of my throat, and I gag.

I pull away to catch my breath for a second but go back in now that I know what to expect. I relax my throat and take as much of him as I can, and I use my hand and mouth in unison for the rest. He fists my hair, thrusting his hips to deepen the angle and increase the tempo.

Saliva spills from the corners of my mouth, but this just adds to the intensity of it.

I relax my throat, and when he hits the back of it, he groans.

"You're going to make me come so fast at this rate."

And I'm so okay with that.

I stroke his shaft and match the rhythm with my mouth. Something is incredibly powerful about this. An alpha like Lenny surrendering this way is a heady aphrodisiac. However, I realize if this were any other man, I would happily bite off their dick and feed it to them.

But Lenny is once in a lifetime, and I know I'm ruined forevermore.

He fucks my mouth harder, faster, and I take it. I bend to his wild thrusts as he pulls my hair, and when I reach down and fondle his balls, he explodes.

He quickly attempts to pull out, but I latch onto his thighs and suck hard. He has no other choice but to come in my mouth.

I swallow happily because we're now forever joined.

The last spasm rocks his cock before he grips my throat and yanks me up. I don't have time to swallow him all, so his cum spills into his mouth from mine. We kiss like starved lovers, both our tastes lingering on the other's lips.

Something I've associated with feelings of hatred and shame has now been replaced with this.

Does that mean I'm "saved"?

As Lenny presses his forehead to mine, no words need to be spoken. We both know this changes everything, but I just don't know if that change is for the good.

CHAPTER 11

LENNY

I like watching her sleep.

I think it's because that's the only time she ever looks at peace.

Last night, she let me in. I know her past contains monsters that feed on her soul every single day, but she let go of her fears and surrendered. She trusted me, which, for us, is something we don't dish out easily.

But now, I don't know what any of this means.

Do we go back to not talking?

Hating one another?

I don't want that, but I also don't want to be weird about it.

If Gianna were to find out about this, I know she'd find a way to make us both pay, and that's the reason I run my fingers down the middle of Valentina's back.

She's lying on her stomach, her face turned to the side. The sheet rests just above her perfect ass. Goose bumps kiss her flesh, reminding me of her sweetness, which lingers on my tongue.

She brushes the hair from her face as she turns to look at me. I instantly smell strawberries.

Something suddenly happens, something that hasn't happened before—my heart begins to beat faster, and my mouth goes dry.

We look at one another, knowing that last night changed everything, but neither of us has been taught how to deal with whatever the fuck this feeling is.

I've been with girls before, but last night, both Valentina and I are virgins when it comes to matters of the heart.

All I know is that I'll protect her and kill anyone who stands in my way.

"Are you all right?" I ask because I know giving herself to me the way she did wasn't easy.

Her past will forever threaten to taint her future, but she trusted me, and for someone who has never trusted anyone her entire life, it only has me wanting to protect her all the more.

She nods, her cheeks blushing.

I wish I could woo her, but regardless of last night, I'm not going to turn into a simp and forget the pressing matters at hand—we need to get the fuck out of here.

"We need to go."

"Go where?"

"I mean leave…like forever leave."

All matters of the heart soon evaporate.

Valentina pulls the sheet over her naked form as she stands. "What are you talking about? This is our home."

"This has never been our home. We need to leave before Gianna—"

"Before Gianna what?" she coaxes, arching a brow.

"Before Gianna reveals her grand plans for us."

Valentina scoffs. "Please, can you be any more dramatic? If it wasn't for her, God knows where we'd be. She took us in when no one else wanted us. She may not have been a loving role model, but she provided for us and made us who we are today."

"Bullshit!" I argue, leaping out of bed. "You're brainwashed. She dangled you like a piece of meat in a tank of starving sharks!"

"It was a test, one which I passed."

"Don't you see? We shouldn't have to continue to pass her fucking tests! This isn't normal. She's training us for something. I don't know for what yet. But I do know that she'll use us in any way that benefits her."

Valentina is angry. Her flushed skin is a dead giveaway.

But she needs to know the longer we stay here, the more danger we're in.

"Come with me. Let's go. Anywhere, I don't care. Just away from here."

I walk toward her, hands raised in surrender because I don't want to fight.

"Why have you stayed then? If you think she's up to no good, why didn't you leave years ago?"

The inevitable question…

"Answer me."

With a sigh, I meet those blue eyes of hers that promise me the world and will rob me of life. "Because I knew you wouldn't come, and I can't leave you here. But I can't stay. I can't stay when I know it'll kill us both."

"Is that why you fucked her?"

"*Who? Gianna?*" I ask, pulling a disgusted face.

She nods firmly.

So that was why she was parading around with NFL Ken—she was jealous. She *did* see Gianna and me together, but she didn't stay around long enough to see how it ended.

"I did nothing of the sort," I reply firmly. "It's all a game. She's a means to an end."

"And what end is that?"

I mull over how much I can tell her, and she reads it loud and clear.

"You don't trust me." It's not a question. It's a statement. "What a fucking idiot I am!"

She storms for the door, but I quickly sidestep, blocking her path.

"Get out of my way!"

But I stand firm.

"Please, just trust me, something bad is coming, and I don't want you here when it happens."

"How do you know that?"

"I can't tell."

"Un-fucking-believable. You expect me to just believe you, all because you made me come? Fuck you."

She shoves me out of the way, but I grip her throat and slam her back against the wall. She fights me. All it does is get me hard.

"I expect you to believe me because deep down, you know I'm right," I say, inches from her face. "Gianna is up to something, and it's only a matter of time until our true purpose is revealed. Please don't be stubborn. It'll get you killed.

"We've been training for a war our entire lives. The war is coming. I know that it is. Please don't be on the other side when it does. Gianna is a fucking drug dealer! You're not stupid. She's a fucking psychopath."

"Or what? You'll kill me? Is that it?" That's what she decides to take from what I've just said. She's not bothered that the money we spend is on the backs of nothing but greed and misery.

Silence…

"You fucking asshole. You give me bits and pieces and expect me to give up my life because you say so? Well, I say no. I'm here because I want to be. I'm here because Gianna has the answers I need."

"Your mom?" I ask because it doesn't take a genius to know that Valentina believes Gianna knows where her mom is.

Like how I did with Lewis, and I was right—she did know.

But she won't hand over that information without offering her something first, and that's what I'm afraid of. What will Valentina have to do for Gianna to get what she wants?

"Nothing in this world is free," I say, never breaking eye contact. "She's trained you to be her little lapdog, and she'll use you any way she wants because she has something you want. She'll ensure you pay dearly for that information."

"Speaking from experience?" she wisely asks. "You think she knows where your brother is, right? That's why you've stayed."

Yes, but I've also stayed for her. But I can't tell her that without making her feel second best.

"Please, just come with me."

It's only a matter of time. I can feel it in my gut. And I can't shake the feeling that it has something to do with Aldo.

"No," she stubbornly states. "Now let me go."

"Why are you loyal to her?"

"Why are you not?"

"Because I don't trust her. The way she raised us, it's not normal. It's like she secluded us from the world for a reason. Like she didn't want us to know what's really out there because it'll reveal who she really is."

"She looked after us, Lenny! She fed us. Schooled us. She taught us how not to be a victim in this world. Before her, that's all I was."

"No, you weren't," I argue, releasing my hold around her neck. "You never were. But she's brainwashed you into thinking you won't survive without her. She needs you, not the other way around."

"Find my mother, then! Get me the revenge I deserve on Father Merry and that fucking orphanage, and then I'll come with you. Until then, I'm staying."

"This isn't just about your mother, is it? You stay because you owe her some sort of loyalty. Why? It's because of her you killed a man without remorse. What will she have you do next?"

Valentina knows I'm right. She too knows that something wicked is coming this way. But she stays because Gianna has the answers we both need. But unlike me, who found Aldo,

Gianna is Valentina's only hope of getting what she wants.

I understand, but I fear what we both must lose to get the answers we seek.

"We can find what we need—together, and away from here."

"Can you promise me that?"

I avert my gaze because I cannot.

"Then get out of my way, Lenny."

"Why do you fight me every chance you get?"

I punch the wall in frustration.

Valentina doesn't flinch. "Because I can."

Every inch of my body protests, but I know no one will surrender today.

She opens the door and slams it behind her as she leaves me alone with my failure.

"Fuck," I curse under my breath.

I knew she'd fight me, but this is worse than I thought.

Gianna has something over both our heads, but unlike me, Valentina doesn't have a plan B.

I'm thinking of ways to make her see the danger she's in when the door opens. I'm hopeful Valentina has come to her senses, but Gianna enters.

I don't have the patience to pretend. "Get out."

Of course, she merely laughs in response. "I failed as a parent."

"You were never a parent, Gianna, so stop with the bullshit.

What do you want?"

She closes the door, leaning against it. "Did you find Lewis?"

I inhale slowly because this is the first time she's used his name. And she's done so with intent.

"The way you're looking at me, anyone would think I didn't give you what you asked for."

"You knew he was a junkie, didn't you?"

Gianna examines her nails casually. "I was only trying to protect you. That's all I've ever wanted for the two of you. But I can see that the time has come for me to let you spread your wings."

"I'm not leaving Valentina here alone with you," I state firmly.

"She's a big girl. She doesn't need you to protect her. She never did."

"What are you planning? Whatever it is, I'm clearly not needed. Therefore, I can only assume you need Valentina to do something you cannot."

Her back straightens because I've hit a nerve. "Choose your words wisely, Lennon."

But she can go fuck herself.

"Or what? You're all talk. If you weren't, then you wouldn't need two kids to do your dirty work. Valentina is everything you're not. I won't let you destroy her."

Gianna's eyes narrow. It seems the ice-cold queen does have

feelings.

I wait for a response, but she simply leaves.

I wish I felt this was a victory, but I know…this is the onset of war.

Aldo is out back doing "stocktake."

I honestly can't believe that I'm back here, dusting a Himalayan salt lamp while listening to what sounds like whales mating to Enya.

But I cannot find anything that hints at this store being anything but a hippie haven.

I refuse to believe I'm wrong, though. Aldo's reputation is infamous among all men. As is Gianna's. And I'm caught between the two.

I know I shouldn't have pushed Gianna, but I'm done. I can't pretend any longer. I can only hope Valentina comes to her senses and thinks over what I said.

I need to uncover the connection between Gianna and Aldo. Yes, they're rivals, but there's something more. There's a reason Aldo came to the orphanage. Valentina is the common denominator.

But why?

"Molto bene."

Aldo's praise snaps me the fuck out of my head.

He looks around the store in what seems like approval. If this is a test, then I think I passed.

"Want to come make a delivery with me?"

I notice he carries a large bag of white crystals.

Of course, I agree.

He locks up, and we walk toward a black Jeep. "No driver today?"

Aldo simply smiles.

We get in, and he punches an address into the GPS. It's an hour away. Once he selects his playlist of classical tunes, we're off.

I don't make small talk.

I wait to be spoken to because this delivery is a test.

"There is a fight organized for tonight."

I nod.

"You don't ask a lot of questions," he says lightly, eyes on the road.

"I didn't think I needed to."

Aldo chuckles. "You're not curious?"

"Not really, no. I know we're not here to waste one another's time."

"You've not told me anything about your brother. I mean, he's the reason you've put your trust in a stranger."

"Oh, I don't trust you," I correct firmly. "And I know you

don't trust me. But I hope to change that soon enough."

"You are a smart young man, Lennon," he says, his accent thick. "I wonder why it is you need me."

"Because you are nothing in this world without someone you can trust. Me, I only trust two people, and one of them is me."

"And the other?"

I don't reply as he knew I wouldn't.

"This is a business proposal we both benefit from. I'm not proposing we become friends, but I think we want the same thing."

"And what's that?"

I mull over his question. I want to be as honest as I can. I need to be because time is of the essence.

"To be the best in every possible way and eliminate anyone who stands in the way."

Aldo doesn't say a word.

When we arrive at a derelict building in the middle of nowhere, I know things are going to get messy.

Whether this is where I prove my loyalty or I'm to be taught a lesson, I don't know.

I follow Aldo, not expecting a single thing. The old factory is a squatter's paradise, but there's no one here…bar the man tied to the wooden chair in the middle of the room.

He's blindfolded, his wrists and feet bound.

"To be the best in every possible way and eliminate anyone who stands in the way," Aldo says, repeating what I said in the car.

Seems I was right after all.

"Sucks to be him," I reply without feeling.

Aldo simply laughs.

Glenn appears from the corner, gun in hand. "He swears he knows nothing."

I assume they're talking about the chump who was stupid enough to find himself in the position he's in.

Aldo casually walks toward the man, giving nothing away. Glenn makes clear he's far from impressed that I'm here.

But my gut tells me something isn't right, and I'm not talking about Glenn's double denim outfit choice.

"Baz, this would be a lot easier if you told us the truth." Aldo takes the blindfold off Baz, who blinks quickly to adjust to the dim light.

"I'm telling you the truth!" Baz implores, begging Aldo to believe him.

"You're full of shit," Glenn counters, coming out of nowhere and pistol-whipping him.

Seems a little excessive, and it must show on my face.

"You have something you wish to say?"

Aldo is asking me this because he too senses something is amiss.

Baz looks between us, clearly unsure of what's going on.

"I'm not sure what you think he did, but he doesn't look like a rat. I mean, he's wearing a fanny pack."

Aldo's lips twitch.

"You're listening to this kid?" Glenn asks, angered.

Aldo's humor soon dies when he turns his attention to Glenn. The room grows smaller, and I soon understand why something is amiss.

Baz was merely the bait...

"Someone is stealing from me," Aldo says, the bag of crystals in his hand. "And Glenn thinks it's you."

"Why would I do that?" Baz cries, shaking his head frantically. "You've been good to me and my family. I don't want any trouble. I keep to my neighborhood and do what you ask."

I look closely at that bag Aldo holds, and an epiphany hits. It's the perfect fucking alibi. I was an idiot not to have guessed sooner.

"Bravo ragazzo."

Aldo reads my thoughts as he passes me the bag.

I shut out all external stimuli and rifle through the stones, feeling for something...different. And when I find one, I know what I have to do.

Pulling it out, I hold it out in front of me, closing one eye to examine it closely. I turn it over and over, looking for the sweet spot. I find it within seconds.

If I'm wrong, then I'm about to look a fool. But as I smash the stone against the wall and a puff of white powder coats my hand, I know I just passed this test.

The crystals are legit; some *are* for healing, while most are transporting drugs because who the fuck would have guessed these harmless stones would hold A-grade cocaine.

But I'm sure each color stone represents a different drug.

This is fucking genius.

"You continue to impress me because someone with passion will do anything to succeed." Aldo reaches into his jacket and retrieves the piece he has in his gun holster.

I don't flinch because I know it's not for me.

He aims the gun on the person this entire theatrical performance is for. "Glenn, I'm disappointed it's ended this way. But someone is stealing from me, and we both know it's not someone as foolish as Baz. No offense."

"None taken," Baz is quick to say, thankful the heat is directed elsewhere.

"This someone has inside knowledge of my business, and we both know Rocco and Ramond are too stupid to pull anything this complex off, so that only leaves you."

"You're fucking serious?" Glenn says, his utter shock

apparent.

I watch for any cues that he's lying.

"Why would I do that?"

"Why does any man betray another? Wealth? Power? Ego? There are endless possibilities. What I do know is my product is being sold over the valley. That's your neighborhood, correct?"

Glenn nods while I'm hit with the truth.

Glenn isn't the one stealing from Aldo.

But Aldo's daughter is.

That's where I first saw her, sneaking out of that crack house where Lewis supposedly is. She knew the valley streets well. It wasn't her first rodeo because she's undercutting her father and profiting from his stuff.

But why?

I'm sure it's not to make a little extra pocket money.

My stomach drops because whatever the reason, I will be the decider of either her or Glenn's fate.

"Yes, but I—"

"Shh." Aldo cuts him off, not interested in excuses. "What do you think, Lennon?"

Glenn beseeches I show mercy.

But how do I do that without throwing Aldo's own daughter under the bus?

And what if I'm wrong?

"I think every man has the right to a fair trial."

"You show him mercy when he wouldn't do the same for you?"

"He and I are nothing alike."

"This is true, but I cannot have a man I do not trust."

"Please, Aldo, you know me. I wouldn't steal from you."

"Yet you lie to me by bringing me Baz when you knew he wasn't involved. How can I trust you?"

Aldo was testing us all.

I passed.

Glenn failed.

"I knew if I didn't bring someone, you'd kill me!" Glenn's desperation shines, and I wonder if perhaps he *is* guilty of something.

Is he working with Aldo's daughter? He knows if he rats her out, he's dead either way.

"If you were merely honest, then things would have ended very differently for you." Aldo's composure reveals why he's in the position he's in.

He earned his title not through fear but rather respect.

But make no mistake, double-cross him, and you'll end up like ole Glenn here.

"Tell me what you know, and all will be well."

"I can't!" Glenn replies, tears in his eyes. "She'll kill me."

"Who will?"

I sigh because Glenn is a dead man walking.

"The person you trust."

Before another word can be spoken, Glenn reaches for the gun in the small of his back, shoves it into his mouth, and blows his brains out.

His headless corpse drops to the ground with a squelch.

It takes Baz a moment to process the scene feet away before he screams hysterically.

My heart pounds uncontrollably. I'm covered in Glenn's brains and blood, but I stand completely still.

Aldo reaches into his pocket and offers me a white handkerchief, which I accept. It is red when I'm done wiping my face with it.

"Egyptian cotton?" I ask, handing it back to him.

He waves me off, indicating I can keep it.

This scene is utterly comical, and that's because this is my norm.

"A position has just opened up," Aldo says, tongue in cheek, turning to look at me. "I need a man I can trust. I don't want you to fight for me. You're too smart for that."

"You trust me?"

Aldo smiles. "Lennon Shepherd, you are far more valuable alive to me than you are dead."

Shit…

He knows my name, which means…he knows who I am.

"You knew who I was this entire time, didn't you?"

"Yes," he replies, not insulting me by lying. "You never questioned my Italian, which made me believe you knew what I was saying. And only one person teaches to fight the way you do. So the question is, are you here to take me down?

"Or could it be...you're here to take *her* down."

This entire time, I thought I was a player in the game, but now I see I was merely on the sidelines, waiting for my turn to play.

"And who is she?" I ask, wondering if I too am about to join headless Glenn.

Aldo smiles, forever the motherfucking king of this kingdom. "Gianna Ricci...the woman who adopted you and *bellezza*. I'm sorry I didn't get there first. I should have known she'd get to her before I could."

"What does she want with her?"

This is the moment I've been waiting for. The answers I've been searching for, for years.

"She is the answer to it all. She has the ability to destroy us all, which means...she is the enemy. You pick a side, Lennon, because there's no going back once you decide."

"I won't leave her there."

"Then bring her here." When he reads my confliction, he guesses why. "But she will not come. Gianna has a way of making one feel as though they'd perish without her."

"How do you know all this?"

Aldo sighs heavily as if reliving a memory that plagues him to this day. "I know Gianna because she is my ex-wife."

My poker face is long gone because what in the ever-living fuck? If Gianna is his ex, does that mean the girl I saw sneaking out of the crack house is her daughter?

This shit just gets more and more fucked up, but I guess it explains a lot because nothing in life is a coincidence.

"I promise your brother will get the help he needs. All I ask in return is you pledge your loyalty to me. But to do that, I need you to do whatever Gianna says. She cannot know anything is amiss."

"And then what happens?"

Aldo appears saddened by what he says next, but all's fair in love and war. "Then I take back what she stole from me. Her empire was built on everything I taught her. I confided in her, I…loved her, and in return, she stabbed me in the back because greed is more important to her than love.

"She has no heart. Trust me when I say this. She will use anyone to get what she wants. There is a war coming, Lennon. And I fear that war is not between me and her. I fear it is between you and Valentina…just the way Gianna intended.

"She has no problems killing me and burning my empire to the ground. But she knows she cannot win. She's tried but has always failed. She's forgotten who taught her everything she knows. Her allies grow tired of her games.

"She needs a new queen, one she can control, one she can trust. New blood is needed. A new leader who can seduce any man to do what she commands."

"Valentina won't leave her. I've tried."

"Then you must try harder."

"Even if I get her to agree, she has an unbreakable loyalty to her. Valentina believes Gianna can help her find her mother and get revenge on the orphanage."

Aldo's face soon changes, and I know why.

"You know where her mother is, don't you?"

He replies after a few moments of silence. "Yes."

"Then tell me, and this can all be over!"

But I soon realize he won't, and that's because nothing in this world is free.

"Prove your loyalty first, and then I shall tell you everything."

"And until then?" I ask, angered because I'm now left with more questions than answers.

He simply smiles. "Until then, we sell crystals."

CHAPTER 12

VALENTINA

I'm envisioning punching Lenny in the face, but I don't feel any better.

It's incredible how easily my emotions can switch when thinking about him.

Love him.

Hate him.

Love him.

How dare he think he can tell me what to do? Just because he made every part of me feel alive doesn't give him the right to dictate what I should or shouldn't do.

But a small, annoying voice screams at me that he's right.

Gianna's behavior has been different lately. It feels as though she's preparing us for something, and when she knocks on my door, it seems I'm about to find out what.

"Are you all right?" she asks, catching me off guard.

I don't remember her ever asking if I'm okay, so why the change of heart?

"Fine," I reply blankly.

She enters and makes clear she has something she wishes to say.

"Valentina, you're at the age now when I can tell you the truth. It's your birthday tomorrow, so I wish to give you a birthday present."

She's right. It touches me she remembered.

"Adopting you wasn't a coincidence," she confesses softly. "I knew your mother."

And just like that, time stands still.

I can't speak, so Gianna continues.

"I knew her because she was once a friend of mine. However, I didn't know your father. Margarette was the first friend I made when I moved here from Sicily. She was so kind to me. She took a chance on me when no one else did."

This trip down memory lane may hold fond memories for Gianna, but this woman she speaks of is nothing but a stranger to me.

"She was volunteering at the church and welcomed me into the parish. I felt like I finally found a place I fit in. But when she met your father, she changed. We tried to make her see reason, but your mother was stubborn, and I see that in you.

"It's why I've pushed you all these years, because I know her blood runs in your veins."

This is…a lot.

From being given no information to now this, I can barely keep up.

"Do you know where she is now?"

Gianna sighs before nodding slowly.

A flood of emotion overwhelms me. She knew this entire time, but she never told me. She never alluded to the fact she knew who I was.

I can't help but feel a stab of betrayal.

"Why did you adopt me?"

Gianna mulls over my question.

"Please," I beg, not caring how weak I sound. I need to know the truth.

"Because she asked me to," she finally confesses, her eyes turning soft. "I didn't know you existed until she wrote me a letter, asking I do this for her."

"And why couldn't she?" I question, angered. "She left me on those steps of that orphanage like I was nothing but garbage, and when she could finally make some sort of amends for that, she asks *you* to do what she should have done!"

I jump up from the bed, pacing the room with my heart in my throat. "Tell me where she is."

When there is silence, I stop in front of Gianna, shaking my head incredulously.

"She doesn't want me to know where she is, does she?"

Gianna frowns, but her silence speaks volumes.

"I cannot believe this. Even now, she still wants nothing to do with me! What did I do?" I cry, tears of anger filling my eyes.

"She can't see you, *piccola*."

"Why the fuck not?" I would never speak to Gianna this way, but all sense of reason is long gone.

"It's best for you to know this and nothing else."

"That's not fair," I spit, shaking my head. "You give me snippets of information and expect that to be enough."

"I'm doing this to protect you," she replies sympathetically. "Your mother doesn't want to see you. But that doesn't mean she doesn't love you. We are doing this to protect you."

"Protect me?" I exclaim. "From what?"

So help me God, if Gianna doesn't explain, I'll tear this house to the ground.

"From the man who is hunting her. His name is Aldo Cattaneo."

And just like that, my purpose in this entire game is finally revealed.

"H-he came to the orphanage. He was going to adopt me, but you did first. You knew he came?"

Gianna nods. "Your mother is still in contact with the sisters at the orphanage. They told her about Aldo. She didn't come herself because she is in hiding. From him."

I don't know what to say or think because this doesn't make sense.

"What did she do to him?"

"She stole from him."

"What did she steal?"

"His heart," she finally reveals. "A lover scorned is a dangerous thing, and someone like Aldo—the most powerful drug dealer in all of the East Coast—that makes him lethal. A man like Aldo has everything he wants, and if he doesn't, he buys it, but he could never buy your mother.

"She left you on those steps to protect you as she had you in secret. If anyone were to find out you existed, they would exploit you. Aldo would use you to smoke out your mother because he's been looking for her for years."

"None of this makes any sense," I confess, stunned beyond words. "Why have you trained me the way you have all these years? And why tell me this now?"

Gianna purses her lips as if weighing up whether she should share more secrets. "Because it's simple—you kill Aldo, you get your mother back. I see I cannot hide the truth from you any longer. You will eventually seek her out. So I would rather tell you than you hurt yourself trying."

I slump onto the end of the bed, fearful my legs won't hold me up. "This entire time, you were training me for this?"

Gianna nods, sitting beside me. I don't think she's ever been this close to me before, and it makes sense. She never adopted me because she wanted a child. She did so as a favor to a friend. If this doesn't prove Gianna's loyalty, then I don't know what does.

This explains why she never treated me as a daughter, and that's because I wasn't.

I was someone else's.

"But getting to Aldo won't be easy. He's never alone. He welcomes the strays and feeds them; he cares for them and earns their trust, but in the end, it's all for his own gain."

Although my memory of him is hazy, I don't remember getting that feeling from him. I thought he was kind. But I guess this correlates with what Gianna is saying.

Aldo is a predator, and a smart one at that.

But there isn't a question about it; Aldo must die, and he must die by my hand.

"Tell me what I have to do."

Gianna smiles and gently brushes the hair from my cheek. A foreign gesture of love, one which she has never done before.

"What have I taught you about love?"

"Love makes you weak. Love will be the death of you," I reply, thinking back to the night all those years ago when Gianna taught Lenny and me a very valuable lesson.

I didn't see it then. But now, I do.

"*Brava, piccola*," she says with affection.

I suddenly crave it more than I thought I knew. I want nothing more than to please her, so I'll do whatever she asks.

"Aldo has a daughter from a previous relationship. Bring her to me, and that'll bring Aldo to you. She is his one and only collateral, which is why I've taught you not to attach."

I know she's speaking about Lenny. I suddenly feel so foolish for ever doubting her.

"What did Aldo do to you?" I ask because we're all game players in this. I just don't understand Gianna's role.

"I want what is his," she declares without pause.

"And what is that?"

"His empire. I'm his rival, *piccola*. Deep down, you knew this all along. This is why I keep to myself and why I have taught you to do the same. We cannot trust anyone, for I fear the time has come when a war must be had. I knew we would be here one day, which is why I've been preparing you. But I fear I have failed with Lenny. He has turned rogue, hasn't he?"

I bite the inside of my cheek because she's right. But no matter what Lenny has done, I can't help but be loyal to him.

I knew Gianna wasn't working a nine-to-five job, but finally knowing what she does, I don't feel disgusted; I feel honored she saw potential in me when no one else did.

"My life isn't normal, but this is my normal. I do not know any other way. This is why I left Sicily. This is why I must protect my empire; the people who want what is mine will stop at nothing until they steal it from under me.

"Aldo's family and mine have been enemies for a very long time. This drug war started in Italy, and I fear it may end there."

"What does that mean?"

"I need someone I can trust to look after business there. I cannot go back. I'm hunted. Which is why I stay here."

I need some time to process this. I never would have guessed this, and now, I understand why Gianna waited for the right time to tell me.

I wasn't ready before.

But now, I am.

The night when I killed that man was a test she laid down for me to see if I was ready. And I proved to her that I am.

"What is it you want?"

She places her hand on my cheek. I lean into it, never realizing how much I need her touch.

"Bring me Aldo's daughter, then I will do the rest. Once Aldo is taken care of, your mother is free."

"And what of your business in Italy?"

She smiles. "I raised you the way I did because I always

intended to offer you a seat in my kingdom."

"You wish for me to go to Italy, then?"

She nods. "But only if that is what you want."

A new life paved with power and control? The temptation is too great to turn down.

But there is one thing holding me back—Lenny.

"Perhaps you and your mother could start a new life?" Gianna says gently, as if reading my hesitation.

A happy reunion is not in the cards just yet because she has eighteen years of explaining to do. But at least I know why she left me even though I don't agree with her choices. But as I see it, Aldo is the reason my life is so fucked up.

I once thought him to be my savior, but now I see, he is a dead man walking.

"And Father Merry?" I question because there's no way he's walking away scot-free.

Gianna places a kiss to my forehead—the first kiss she's ever given me. "You take them all, *piccola*. It's what you were born to do. Happy birthday."

CHAPTER 13

LENNY

Time is of the essence, more so than ever, now that I know the truth.

I wanted to wait, but I can't.

Aldo knows someone is stealing from him, but he just doesn't know it's his own flesh and blood. And this is the upper hand I need to get answers about my brother.

I don't even know her name. But what I do know is that she's trouble, which is why I followed her home.

It's late, and after the shit I learned today, I really need to get back to Valentina. Aldo wants me to play nice with Gianna, but I'm not sure how long that shit will fly before I tell her to go fuck herself.

But if Valentina continues to fight me, I don't know what I'll do.

I choose a side, and that's Aldo's. I don't know why, but I trust him.

Once this is done, I could always attempt to live a normal life, but the bloodlust in me shakes its head, knowing I don't play nice with normalcy. I'm too far gone for that.

Perhaps, I gravitated toward Aldo because he has something I admire—respect.

He isn't a good guy, I know that. And although I'm fucking opposed to drugs, they're going to be dealt one way or another. Whether I deal them or not, people are going to get fucked up. If we sell good product that's not cut with shit, then maybe that'll save them from the inevitable.

Nice try, I tell myself because there is no way to justify being a drug dealer. I just have to accept that I'm not an honorable man.

Aldo's daughter slips from the apartment. I wonder if Aldo lives here. I also wonder if Gianna is her mother.

Fuck me, this is an HBO documentary dream.

I keep to the shadows, watching her closely. She carries an air of confidence on her shoulders, perhaps even arrogance, which will get her caught.

I have no idea why she would need to steal. Money wouldn't be an issue. So I'm guessing she's doing it as a fuck-you to Aldo. Perhaps she is Gianna's daughter after all.

She clutches the straps of her backpack tightly, no doubt to protect what's inside.

How can Aldo not know his own daughter is stealing from him? I guess love makes you do crazy things, something that Gianna taught us from day one.

Aldo's daughter turns down an alley, and it's not to feed the stray cats. I slow down and stick close to the wall. Peering around it, I watch the transaction take place as she reaches into her backpack and gives the guy a small bag.

He eyes it hungrily as he tosses a rolled-up stack of bills at her.

This is small fry. I'm a little disappointed. But she's smart as she knows anything bigger, and her father would be onto her. Little does she know he already is. I snap a few photos on my phone because it'll be her word against mine. So I now have the proof I need.

The guy scurries off while she places the money into her boot.

Now is my time to strike.

I don't mask my footsteps as I approach her. She spins, and it takes a few seconds before she recognizes me.

"You," she says, not bothering to mask her disgust. "Are you following me?"

"Yes," I deadpan.

She's taken aback by my honesty, and her confidence is soon replaced with suspicion. "Who are you?"

"My name is Lennon, and I guess I work for your dad now. Although I use the word work very loosely."

She doesn't need me to explain further. She knows she's in deep shit.

"What do you want?"

Folding my arms across my chest, I weigh over her request. "Your name first."

She sighs heavily, clearly not amused by small talk. "Bria."

"Well, it's lovely to make your acquaintance, Bria. I won't waste either of our time. I know you're stealing from your dad and selling his stuff."

When she opens her mouth, ready to argue, I hold up a hand, stopping her.

"I know that you are, so please don't bullshit me. This will be a lot easier on us both if we're honest with one another."

Bria mulls over my comment before saying, "All right then, what the fuck do you want? Money? I have a lot of that, so name your price."

"I don't want your money." I shake my head before adding, "And I don't want that either."

She looks relieved I'm not going to ask her to blow me in

his filthy alley.

"Then what?"

"The crack house you were dealing at in the valley, I need you to take me there."

"Why?" She gives me a once-over, curiosity clear because I don't look like her typical clientele.

"The less we know about one another, the better."

"Well, to be fair, I know jack shit about you, and you seem to know a lot about me, so I'm not telling you anything until you give me something."

I mull over her request. It's a fair one. "I think one of your clients is my brother."

She waits for the punchline, but there is none.

When she realizes I'm done, she shakes her head. "I hate to break it to you, but there a lot of brothers inside that hellhole, but the person you remember is no longer there. Trust me. He checked out the moment he became a junkie.

"He would sell your own mother for his next fix."

"She's the reason he's like this."

Bria folds her arms across her chest. "No, Lennon, *he's* the reason he's the way he is. No one forces him to sniff or inject the shit that he does. So stop trying to save someone who doesn't want to be saved. Trust me, this will only get you hurt."

"Gee, thanks for the pep talk, but no one asked you. So mind your fucking business." Her attitude is pissing me off.

She doesn't know me. Or Lewis. She knows jack shit about our situation.

I'm going to save Lewis…even if he doesn't want me to.

Bria reads my stance and shrugs. "Don't say I didn't warn you. Your brother—"

But I'm done talking.

I grip her throat and slam her body into the wall. When she tries to break free, I shove her harder, her back slamming into the bricks. I tighten my grip around her throat.

"Look, I don't care about you. I'm not interested in what you have to say. You're simply a means to an end. I have no issues telling your dad what I know. But hey, I'm a nice a guy and thought I would give you the benefit of the doubt and hope we could work something out.

"But you're really starting to piss me off. So either you do as I've asked or we can go our separate ways right now. It's your choice."

Her eyes are filled with fire, and I have no doubt she's envisioning ways of making my death look like an accident, but I don't have time for this shit. I'm not here to make friends. I need to find Lewis and then convince Valentina that Gianna is Satan reincarnate.

Bria eventually concedes, much to her disgust. I do admire the fight in her.

Cautiously, I let her throat go, never breaking eye contact

with her as a warning that if she tries any shit, I will make good on my word.

When she's free, she shoves me in the chest, making her contempt for me more than clear.

I simply chuckle in response.

She leads the way, and we walk in silence, both of us wanting this over with.

No one bothers us because, let's face facts, we're the ones who would fuck shit up. Everyone keeps to themselves in this part of town anyway. A haven for those who just want to disappear and not belong.

It's a dark night; even the moon doesn't want to come out and witness the shit about to go down.

"What does he look like?" Bria says, breaking the silence.

Her voice is almost alien-like out here in the quiet. But we both know it's the quiet before the storm.

She reads my hesitation for what it is—I don't know what the grown-up Lewis looks like. "Fucking great. A name, then?"

"Lewis."

The falter to her step confirms my worst fears.

I don't know what I'm about to walk into, but it won't be good.

When we approach the house, I stop and take a moment to appreciate it because it would have been quite a sight in its heyday. This three-story Victorian mansion would have been the envy of many back in the day.

Now, however, it's rotting away; its dilapidated state is a reminder that nothing lasts forever. Regardless of this, though, the impressive home still stands tall at the end of a long dirt driveway. The surrounding cornfields just add to the eerie vibe.

Under different circumstances, I could appreciate the macabre sight, but now, this place is merely a reminder of what my brother has become.

I follow Bria as she walks toward the home, not surprised that a soul isn't out here. I am surprised, however, when she detours around the back.

She reads my hesitation instantly. "Don't say I didn't warn you."

I prepare myself for anything, but when I see what looks like a once guesthouse, I realize I probably can never prepare for this. There is no door, so we walk in and are greeted with what can only be described as hell on earth.

Countless candles are scattered around the room, providing a warm glow for the inhabitants to shoot up and pass out in an ethereal bubble, forgetting the world exists outside this place.

Bria steps over the bodies strewn out on the dirty carpet, strung out on whatever shit they've ingested. The fact they're so subdued hints at heroin.

Lewis can't be here.

The people we step over are someone's brother, sister, father, or mother, but they chose this lonely path that only ever ends in misery. I wonder what led them here.

I wonder a lot of things.

The vibe gets darker the farther we venture. It smells of stale beer, piss, and sex. The orange hue from the candles just adds to the macabre ambience. It feels like I'm awaiting a jump scare from a B-horror movie.

Bria stops just outside a room, hinting she has no intention of holding my hand.

Taking a composing breath, I enter the room. My eyes take a moment to adjust because, if possible, it's even darker in here. But as I see a young man slumped against the wall with a tourniquet tied tightly around his arm and a needle hanging from his limp fingers, I realize this vision will forever be entwined in darkness because that young man is my brother.

I'd recognize that shaggy blond hair anywhere. But it's now clumped together in a dirty mess. He was always skinny, but now, he's nothing but skin and bones.

"It's him?" Bria asks from behind me, her voice the only thing that forces me to believe this nightmare as real.

I nod, never taking my eyes off Lewis.

"We gotta go. Now." The urgency in her voice hints this scene isn't the worst of it.

Dropping to a squat in front of Lewis, I remove the needle from his fingers and throw it into the corner of the room where ten others just like it are piled.

His head is drooped to his chest. A strand of saliva dangles from his chin. How the fuck did he end up here? Not in this shithole, but rather, why did he choose this path for himself?

Or perhaps he was always destined for this life. The apple doesn't fall far from the tree.

The saying rings true: life fucking sucks.

I lift his chin. "Lewis, can you hear me? It's me. It's Lennon."

He's out cold. The only thing alerting me that he's alive is the shallow rise and fall of his chest. Suddenly, anger outranks my sadness.

"Wake the fuck up!" I slap his cheek—hard.

A groan slips past his cracked lips. But he still doesn't come to.

"You're going to have to carry him."

"What the fuck is your hurry, Bria?" I yell over my shoulder, wishing I could control my temper because this isn't her fault.

"Because I don't particularly want to be here when his mack daddy comes back."

Every part of my body pulses in utter rage.

"He's turning tricks. What the fuck!" I punch the wall, my fist going straight through it.

But it's not enough. Nothing will suffice until I kill every person who had a hand in my brother's demise. Because although he's alive, he's dead inside. And I'm afraid he'll never see the light again.

Gianna knew he was here the entire time, so as I see it, she'll also pay in ways unimaginable. But for now, I need to get him the fuck out of here.

He weighs next to nothing, and when I lift him, all I feel are bones. He smells putrid.

Bria's eyes are wide, and she appears frozen in time. I recognize the look.

"It's too late to feel guilty now."

She shakes her head as if attempting to shake away the reality of the role she played in the lives she destroyed.

With Lewis in my arms, we quickly make our way down the hallway. I don't care what or who I stand on. No one is getting in my way ever again.

As we turn the corner, it seems my affirmation is about to be put to the test.

"Bria?" snarls a man who can only be described as utter white trash. I hate using labels, but this redneck is every stereotype rolled into one pile of human shit.

His attention soon wavers from Bria to me, then down to Lewis in my arms. He removes the toothpick from between his lips—I vow to impale it into his eyeball and use it in my martini; I chuckle at the visual.

"Do we have a problem, son?" he asks, staring me down.

"Nope," I reply, popping the P.

I attempt to shove past him, but he uses his arm as a barricade when he slams his hand against the wall. "Now I know you don't think you're taking my property with you."

I close my eyes and exhale slowly. I need a moment.

"He is not anyone's *property*," I say, reopening my eyes and glaring at the motherfucker.

He reads this for what it is—a fight until one of us is dead, which suits me just fine.

"I don't know who you are. And I don't care. But put it back where you found it and get the fuck outta 'ere." He looks at Lewis like he's nothing but dirt.

I stand perfectly still even though every part of me wants to burn down this fucking world and throat fuck it.

"Are you deaf? I said—"

"I heard you." I cut him off because I don't want to give this asshole any more airtime.

He waits for the punchline, but there is none. What there is, however, is a punch…of a different kind.

With Lewis still in my arms, I don't wait for a theatrical moment because there is none. I step forward, and without delay, I headbutt the asshole right between the eyes. I catch him unawares, and he wavers on his feet, which is my chance to toss Lewis onto the floor and dive on top of this fucker and commence beating the living hell out of him.

I connect with every part of his face, taking great satisfaction in hearing his nose crack and the back of his head slam into the floor each time I punch him in the fucking face.

But it's still not enough.

Wrapping my hands around his throat, I begin choking him. I squeeze so hard, I feel his neck spasming as he struggles for air. He soon realizes this is a fight for his life. He slaps at my hands, attempting to buck me off, but I have a firm grip and am pinning him down with my body weight.

He's not going anywhere.

"You're killing him!" Bria screams, and I fucking love the surge of adrenaline that courses through me.

"That's kinda the point," I flippantly reply.

It's intoxicating, and it only has me squeezing harder.

I watch him closely, intrigued as his face turns beet red and his eyes appear glass-like as they almost pop from his head. Humans are a disgusting breed. I can honestly say that I've not met any, bar one, who I like.

My body begins to vibrate, and I suddenly feel myself getting hard. In fact, the more he gasps for breath, the harder I get. I do something that proves the line of humanity was crossed long ago when I release my hold around his neck.

He gasps for air, his mouth opening and closing like a fish out of water. I give him a false sense of security, only to rip it away as I make good on my promise and reach for a rusted nail and ram it into his eyeball.

His toothpick was lost in the scuffle, so this is a good substitute.

His guttural screams are a sign of the pain he's in, and I take great pleasure in knowing I'm the one who is his torturer. It comes naturally to me; a natural-born killer. I suppose I didn't realize how much Gianna's teaching has become ingrained into who I am. Because I feel absolutely nothing as I wrap my hands around his neck one final time and never let go until he takes his last breath.

I never break eye contact with him because I wish for my face to be the last thing he sees as he leaves this earth.

With one final squeeze, I let go and peer down at my hands. I turn them over and now see them in a new light, for they have killed, and I fear it won't be the last time I have blood on them.

I know this is only the beginning of things to come.

Coming to a stand, I see Bria feet away, a hand covering her mouth. "What have you done?"

I don't have time for her melodramatics and pick up Lewis, who is still out for the count. I can't take him to Gianna's. I also don't want to involve Aldo in my mess.

"You've started a war," Bria says, shaking her head.

"It started a long time ago," I correct. "And I'm here to end it. Your secret is safe with me, Bria. But a word of warning, your father knows someone is stealing from him. It's only a matter of time. Consider our debt settled."

And with that, I leave behind the chaos I created with nothing but a smile.

CHAPTER 14

VALENTINA

"You cannot enter without being searched. So please leave all personal belongings behind. Empty your pockets and take off your shoes."

I untie the laces of my scuffed Converse on autopilot because these were not the words I expected to hear when meeting my mother for the first time. But I suppose visiting her at Orchard Parks State Hospital wasn't on the agenda either.

I don't know how to feel. All of this is so surreal. I've been waiting for this moment for what feels like my entire life, and now that it's finally here, I wonder if I should come back another day. I'm not ready. But I doubt I ever will be.

When Gianna gave me this address, I thought I would find closure in some ways, but all I have are more questions. Why is my mother in here? And for how long? But the most important question is why?

"It's okay, sweetie," says the nurse in white. She must be able to read my confliction at being here. "She's having a good day today. She's just had her meds, so she might be a little sleepy, but I'm sure she'll be happy to see you."

I highly doubt that.

I give the nurse my shoes and backpack. My pockets are empty.

I walk through some fancy metal detector, which seems a little excessive, but I guess this sets a precedent of things to come. I'm given a pair of flimsy slippers once I clear security.

"You can't wear laces," the guard says blankly like he's said it a hundred times before.

It takes me a second to realize why.

I always thought my mother was better off. That she was off living some lavish life while I was a prisoner in every sense of the word. But as I'm escorted down the sterile white hallway, my slippers sliding across the polished floors, it seems we were both held against our will.

This is Aldo's fault. That's all I can think. Every story needs a villain, and once upon a time, I thought it was my mother.

But I now see that she too is a victim like me. Although I don't agree with her abandoning me, I can understand why she did it.

In her warped way, she thought she was protecting me. She thought she was leaving me in the care of the men and women she considered family.

This is so fucked up.

The orderly stops in front of a white door. There is a sliver of glass for one to peer in or out. What a sad sight for one to view the world through. He unlocks the door and opens it, stepping aside. He reads my apprehension and shakes his head.

"It's okay. She can't get out."

Instantly, I have visions of repeatedly slamming the door against his face as I pin him in the doorjamb. But I simply nod.

I enter cautiously.

My heart is in my throat. I don't ever remember being this nervous. The room is larger than I thought it would be. It's furnished with the bare minimum and no personal effects. It's a sterile white box. Pushed against the wall is a single bed and strapped to it is a woman.

There is no blanket. No pillow. She lies on plastic. A blue hospital gown drapes her small frame. Her feet are bare.

This is my mother? This is the woman I dreamed about since I was a little girl.

The door shuts behind me, startling me. The orderly waits outside, however, as I can see his head through the tiny pane of glass.

I wipe my sweaty hands against the front of my jean shorts. My mouth is dry. This all feels like a dream.

The woman doesn't seem to know I'm here. She simply stares up at the ceiling, not moving. The leather restraints around her wrists and ankles prohibit her from moving. I want to remove them because she deserves more than being locked up like some rabid animal.

A sadness suddenly swarms me, and tears fill my eyes. I quickly wipe them away with the back of my hand.

Taking a deep breath, I walk toward the bed. I smell disinfectant. My mother still doesn't move a muscle. She's in some sort of comatose state. What medication is she on for her to be so...zombielike? How is this helping her?

My legs feel like they're caught in quicksand the closer I get. But I persevere until I'm standing by her bedside. This is what I've been waiting for my entire life. To meet the woman who gave me life only to take it away when she abandoned me.

It's hard not to be angry, regardless of the circumstances.

Her head is shaved unevenly. The unhealthy shade of her pale skin has me guessing she hasn't seen the sun in a very long time. She looks emaciated. Suddenly, my anger is replaced with pity. It's hard to be mad at someone who looks so helpless.

I'm so conflicted.

She barely blinks, but when she does, it's a delayed reaction.

It seems as though her world plays in slow motion.

I wonder what she sees.

I clear my throat. "Hi."

As far as the first words spoken to your long-lost mother, this is lamer than lame.

She doesn't move. She's barely breathing.

I didn't come here to quit, so regardless of the fact I don't know if she can hear me or not, I speak the words I've wanted to say for so many years.

"Do you know who I am? I'm your daughter. I'm Valentina, but that wasn't the name you chose. It was a name given to me."

I suddenly wonder what she would have named me if our circumstances were different.

"Why did you abandon me? What did I do?" I ask, my lower lip trembling. "Gianna told me what happened. You could have come back, but you left me to rot. Do you know the things…" I pause, composing myself. "Do you know the things they did to me? They were things no child should ever have to endure. This is your fault."

Anger surpasses any emotion as I remember all the times I was forced to do things I never wanted to do.

"It hurt," I whisper, a tear sliding down my cheek. "It hurt a lot. I was five years old when he took my virginity. I was a fucking baby! You were supposed to protect me, but you left me with him! Father Merry!"

Something happens when I say his name—a breath catches in my mother's throat.

My own breath is heavy as I wait for something, anything. I wait for her to snap the hell out of this coma and give me the answers I deserve.

"Margarette!" I cry, a surge of anger coursing through me as I slap her cheek. "Wake the fuck up and own up to the shit you did!"

I slap her other cheek, blinded by rage.

She doesn't have the right to switch off the things she did. No, I won't let her.

"Wake up! Wake up! Wake up!" I scream over and over, a slap to the cheeks following each word.

Her body is lax, but that doesn't stop me from slapping her.

I hate her.

I fucking hate her.

"You're nothing but a coward! You've hidden away all these years, not having to deal with the shit that you've done! I'm ashamed to be your daughter. But finally meeting you, I know I'm nothing like you. Perhaps I'm just like my father, then. And you know what, I'd rather be like him than be a pathetic coward like you."

Yes, baby girl, the apple doesn't fall far from the tree...give her what she deserves.

My father's voice echoes in my head, louder this time.

I'm his daughter. He killed without remorse. He did so time and time again. I think back to when I killed that vile scum of the earth and how I felt absolutely nothing. Taking a life was easy, and when I look down at my mother, I realize I can do it again without a second thought.

I wrap my hands around her throat and squeeze hard. I expect her to jolt to life like a monster from a bad horror movie, but she simply lies still. She doesn't fight, and a part of me wonders if she would if she could.

Perhaps she knows she deserves this. Maybe she knew it would always end this way. Poetic justice, really.

Her eyes are an empty hole, reflecting the empty vessel that is her soul. Just as I tighten my grip, I'm yanked off her by a pair of arms. Like a rabid dog being robbed of her meal, I kick and scream, adamant to finish the job because she doesn't deserve to live.

She doesn't deserve a single shred of compassion because, where was mine?

"Calm down, or we'll have no choice but to call the police," the orderly warns as he tightens his hold around me.

I laugh in his face. "And say what? She's already a fucking corpse! Look at her! She doesn't move! She can't even fucking speak to me! She owes me an explanation!"

"She cut out her tongue. That's why she can't speak!" the orderly exclaims, shaking me still.

"*What?*" I ask, the fight in me dying.

"She clearly doesn't want anyone to know the secrets she guards. Or maybe she knows what will happen if those secrets are ever told. You need to leave now and never come back."

I suddenly feel like I've kicked a puppy. Disgust overcomes me.

The orderly slowly releases me, but he doesn't have to worry—I'll never be back. I will never get the answers I seek. It's only me in this world, and no one will stand in my way.

I found my mother. She turned out to be a huge disappointment.

But I will not dwell on something that is broken and cannot be fixed. However, I will focus on things that I can fix, which is making those who played a part in my pain pay.

Father Merry. And Aldo.

The two men who are already dead…they just don't know it yet.

I've found such peace in the darkness.

I was never afraid of the things that went bump in the night because I've danced with the monsters since childhood. I've seen it all. I've lived through it. But today, meeting my mother proved that I'm now a monster, the thing that people are afraid of.

Gianna wasn't home when I returned. A small part of me was disappointed that a birthday cake wasn't awaiting me. But I soon quashed those thoughts. My life will never be like that.

So here I sit in the woods, alone under the star-filled sky a year older.

Am I wiser, though?

Eighteen years old. I feel eighty.

I'm so tired, but it's beyond fatigue. It's the state I live in. I don't think I'll ever be rested because my mind never switches off. Neither does my heart.

Lenny is the only person who ever cared for me, so it hurts he's not here to wish me a happy birthday. Pathetic, I know.

I don't know where he is. But I do know that he and I will soon be worlds apart. We fight for different sides. Gianna gave me what I asked for, so I'll do the same for her.

Aldo's daughter.

I will do so with great pleasure as it hurts the man who will ultimately die by my hand. But I plan on torturing him first. And what better way than taking away from him what he took away from me?

Family.

I will destroy everything he cares for, ensuring he knows I'm the one who tore down his empire and killed every single thing he loved.

This is the only thing that gives me joy—violence and

bloodshed.

Tipping my face to the heavens, I close my eyes and bask in the silence because tomorrow, I will be surrounded by nothing but chaos.

"Happy birthday."

And just like that, my heart begins to beat once again.

I don't move. I simply just exist in this rare moment of stillness where everything fits.

Lenny stands by my side, but he doesn't crowd me. He never does.

I wonder where he's been.

"Open your hand."

I do as he says.

When he places what feels like a stone attached to a chain on my palm, I open my eyes, curious to see what it is. It's a silver necklace with a small black gem.

It's beautiful.

He gestures that he will put it on for me.

I give it back to him and lift my hair as he stands behind me. "It's a black obsidian," he explains, placing the chain around my neck. "It's for power, protection, and grounding."

He fastens the clasp, his fingers brushing against my skin.

I shiver in response.

I wait for him to remove his fingers, but he doesn't, and it surprises me. "It's also supposed to keep negative energies away and to give one the courage to face their inner truths."

There's a hidden meaning behind his words.

"Are you ready to face yours?"

He brushes a finger along the slope of my neck to across the top of my shoulder. I hold my breath, anticipating his next move.

"Please come with me."

Our time, it seems, has come to an end, which means Lenny has found what he was looking for; he's found his brother. Seems ironic that I too have found my mother. But the answers we sought haven't given us peace.

It's only roused the sleeping dogs who are hungry for war.

"Why ask questions you know the answers to?"

"Because I'm hoping I'm wrong for once."

I scoff, unable to conceal my disgust at his arrogance.

"Whatever you need to find peace, we can do it together, out of here. Please, Valentina."

His sincerity is evident. But it doesn't change a thing. He has his demons to conquer. And I have mine.

"You know," he says, something shifting in his voice, "I can always make you."

Before I can tell him to go fuck himself, he glides his hand around the front of my neck, clasping it tightly. He is still behind me, so I'm trapped. The heat of his body pressed to mine is almost suffocating, but I welcome it.

"You can always try," I reply, barely able to swallow with how tight he holds me. "But we both know you'll lose."

"What makes you so sure?" He slowly forces my head back so we're looking at one another.

The moment is heavy with violence and sex.

"Because of your feelings for me."

It's the first time I've expressed it, but it's not because I'm unsure. I know he feels for me what I do for him. I've never said anything because it doesn't change a thing.

He doesn't say a word, but the fire is stoked behind those smoldering eyes.

"Father Merry has taken more breaths than he deserves. I will be visiting him very soon. I've been biding my time because the surprise in his eyeballs when I gouge them from his head and feed them to him will be worth the wait."

I inhale slowly, savoring the memory I cannot wait to make.

"I'll help you. You don't need Gianna."

"Grow up, Lenny," I scold, narrowing my eyes. "How do we deal with the police? The sisters? The many witnesses who will likely see us? We need someone who is above the law."

Something passes over him, which makes me believe he knows someone else. But when he doesn't share who, I realize this is another reason I can't trust him—because he doesn't trust me.

Perhaps it's because we're fighting to be top dog, which is

why we'd never work—in every single way.

"When I leave here, I'll be the enemy. Gianna will hunt me down…as I will her."

"I don't understand why you hate her."

"Because everything she's done is to benefit herself. She doesn't care about either of us. She will use us as her pawns in the war she wages because she's nothing but a greedy, callous bitch. Why can't you see that!"

He tightens his hold on my throat, his frustrations at breaking point. And I like it.

"She's a leader. And she isn't afraid whose feelings she hurts to get what she wants. I admire her."

I know what my words are doing to Lenny, which is why I have chosen them. The angrier he gets…the harder it is to breathe.

"Admire her?" he scoffs angrily. "I pity you both, then."

"Save your pity for someone who gives a fuck what you think."

Lenny tongues his cheek before exhaling heavily.

It seems our war is about to start early.

With his hand still tight around my throat, he uses the other to quickly unfasten the button on my jean shorts. I don't insult either of us by pretending to fight against something we both want.

He shoves his hand into my underwear, finding me wet

as he slides two fingers into my pussy. I moan the moment he starts fingering me because I want this.

I want him.

I'm lightheaded from what his deft fingers are doing as well as the fact that he is siphoning off my air supply. He is violating me brutally, yet I want more.

"You can't live without me," he cockily states, and even though he's right, I would never admit it. "We are joined, and that'll never change."

"You think because you can get me off, I'm going to be a pathetic groupie," I wheeze, leaning back, relishing his hard body pressed to mine. "Yes, sir. No, sir. Three bags full, sir. Fuck you, Lenny. I don't need you."

He snarls like a rabid dog, punishing me hungrily as he inserts another finger, stretching me wide.

"Your pussy begs to differ, sweetheart."

"Shh, it's hard to pretend you're someone else when you talk."

He releases my throat, and the much-needed gasp of air I take is in vain because I'm robbed of breath when he tears the strapless top from my body and begins kneading my breasts. With his fingers in my pussy, he rubs his thumb over my nipple, heightening everything tenfold.

He is everywhere, yet it's still not enough.

I shimmy my shorts down my legs and kick them off. Next,

I want the underwear off too, but Lenny tsks me.

"We're done. Happy birthday." He removes his fingers and stops touching me, and I swear to God I want to die.

He turns to leave, but hell no.

I yank on his arm and spin him around to face me, slapping his cheek.

We're both breathless, the air between us electric, threatening to shock us both.

He clenches his jaw. "Do that again. I dare you."

I do one better, and I punch him in the face, splitting his lip open.

He touches his mouth, the back of his hand coming away with blood. A smirk slowly spreads across those luscious lips.

I win…

He grabs the back of my neck and forces me to my knees, frantically unfastening his jeans. When his cock springs free, he shoves it into my eager mouth. I gag when it hits the back of my throat. I try to pull away, but he won't let me. He continues to force himself down my throat, fucking my mouth.

He never lets go of the back of my head as he continues to mouth fuck me. I'm so turned on, every part of my body feels like it's on fire. I relax my throat and take him as far as I can. Spit drips from the corners of my mouth because Lenny's cock is huge.

He uses my mouth how he pleases. I'm his fuck doll, and

he's mine because the minute he lets me go, I'm going to ride him until he fucking breaks.

He yanks me off his cock so I can breathe before forcing me back onto his shaft. I grip his upper thighs and suck his dick until he violently pushes me away with a growl. He tugs me up under the arms and slams his mouth over mine.

I taste blood.

Nothing is gentle about this kiss. I pull his hair. He slaps my ass. But the mutual respect of our boundaries is never crossed because I want this as much as him.

He bites my lip and pulls my hair to angle my face so he can mouth fuck me with his tongue just as he did with his dick.

I'm dizzy from lack of oxygen. But I know, more so, I'm breathless because of what the man who I have loved since I was a child is doing to my heart and soul.

I don't want to love him, but I do.

There never was a moment when we "fell in love." I think Lenny and I were always destined to be one. But that doesn't mean a fairy-tale ending is headed our way. This changes nothing. But he wants to be the first man I welcome into my body because I want him.

And I always will.

I pull away, rubbing my thumb over his bloody lip. Mixed with our saliva, I run my thumb down his face, leaving a bloody streak of war paint behind; something I've done many times before. He looks fucking brutal.

It's a frenzy of hands as we tear off our clothes, and the moment we're naked, he tosses me onto the grass and lays on top of me. He doesn't insult me by asking if I'm sure. Or feeling if I'm ready.

I want to be fucked by the boy who stole my heart the moment he crushed it when we were children. We were always destined for this.

He yanks my arms above my head and interlaces our fingers as he thrusts into me.

I hold my breath because he is so deep.

He doesn't move.

He allows me to adjust to his size.

I feel like I'm being split right down the middle…and I love it.

He reads my body and begins to move, his cock and my pussy hungrily fucking because this isn't lovemaking. And I never wanted it to be.

Lenny and I are one and the same, which is why things will always be like this.

We fight.

We fuck.

And then we leave.

Repeat.

Tonight is just the start of what our future holds.

He fucks me hard and fast. I raise my hips and bow my back, taking everything he gives. Yes, it hurts. But it hurts so good.

This is a memory I will cherish, replacing the ones I never wanted to make. For as I see it, Lenny is my first because the monsters before him were not men but vile animals who don't deserve a second thought.

But there is one man who will pay dearly for his sins.

The thought of Father Merry has me meeting Lenny's thrusts and bouncing back on his cock. He looks into my eyes, and I know he sees it, so he slams his mouth to mine and kisses me with nothing but love.

I'm restrained by his body and hands, but I don't feel claustrophobic.

I feel safe.

Twigs and rocks are embedded into my back and ass, causing scrapes that I can feel are bleeding.

I widen my legs, welcoming Lenny to fuck me deeper, but in one swift movement, he flips me onto all fours and sinks back into me, taking me from behind.

A guttural scream rips from my throat because he is tearing me right down the seams. He slaps my ass, holding my hips as he thrusts into me deeply.

"We were never taught love, only hate, but this is the closest thing to it, *tesoro mio*. You will always belong to me. Always.

But I cannot promise that I won't hurt you if you stand in my way."

I bounce back onto his cock, my fingernails digging into the ground as I attempt to anchor myself before I float away. "You can always try."

He slaps my ass again, harder this time, angered that I continue to fight him. "You know I don't like to lose."

"You've already lost," I pant, pushing past the pain. "You could never hurt me...and you know it."

Lenny pulls my hair, forcing my neck back at a painful angle. He doesn't stop thrusting into me, using my hair as reins as he steadies me with a hand on my hip. He is in complete control, and I surrender.

He spreads my ass cheeks, opening me wide, and I scream, never feeling so full.

"*Questo sara sempre mio.* Say it!" he orders, sinking in and out of me slowly, wishing me to feel every hard inch.

I close my eyes as it's almost too much, and I don't want to come yet.

"Say it!" he repeats, grabbing my arms and pinning them behind my back.

He holds on tight as I bounce back on his cock. I'm suspended against him, trusting him not to let me go.

But I know he won't.

When I don't do as he demands, he suddenly stops moving

but never withdraws his cock. I wiggle my ass, desperate for him to continue.

He doesn't.

"Lenny," I moan, my body convulsing and missing the friction.

"Say. It," he orders again, making it clear he won't do what I ask unless I do the same.

I shift my hips, fucking him myself, but he seizes my waist, stopping me. He presses his chest to my back and whispers into my ear, "If you don't say it, I'll make you watch me fuck someone else, *tesoro mio*."

The threat stirs an anger so great, an animalistic growl gets caught in my throat.

He begins to pull out, and the thought of losing him in every way has me surrendering.

"I'm yours—always."

"And?" he coaxes, beginning to slowly fuck me.

He ensures I can feel every hard inch as he pulls out, only to slide back in with ease.

I don't want to say it, but I realize this may be my only chance.

He once again fucks me hard, leaning down and tearing at the skin on my throat. He's marking me, and I fucking love it.

He turns my cheek to smash his lips to mine so I can taste the bloodlust spilling into my very soul. It rouses the demons, and I cry, *"E ti amo!"*

The moment I say those words, I can't take them back. But they didn't have to be said to be real. I've always loved Lenny and will continue to do so until I take my last breath.

He reaches around and begins playing with my clit—it's too much.

He fucks me so hard, the sound of our flesh slapping sends the creatures of the night into hiding. But when I finally come with a sated moan, I know we've roused the monsters who are ready to come out and play.

Game on...

CHAPTER 15

LENNY

H e just sleeps.

And sleeps.

Perhaps it's because it's the first time he's felt safe enough to do so.

Lewis is now sixteen years old, but I barely recognize the boy in this motel bed as my brother.

After I threw his ass in the shower and scrubbed him clean, I put him to bed and told him to sleep because he was safe.

That was three days ago.

But soon, he'll wake as he'll be jonesing for his next hit.

Aldo gave me some drugs to help with the withdrawal, but it seems fucking pointless to mask one addiction with another.

When the door opens, I reach for my piece on the coffee table, but when I see it's Bria, I chill the fuck out. She's not here to hurt us.

She tosses a bag of fast food in front of me. The smell turns my stomach, but I appreciate the sentiment.

"You have to eat something," she says, locking the door behind her.

"Last I checked, my mom burned in a fire. But thanks."

She rolls her eyes, not bothered by my morbid sense of humor because she has one too. She sits beside me, offering me a beer from the six-pack. Now this is more my language.

We drink in silence, both watching Lewis sleep soundly.

I've had this stupid idea that won't go away. I told Bria about Gianna. She thankfully put to rest the notion that Gianna isn't her mom—the world doesn't need her offspring in it. But Bria has balls. She's also fucking smart.

And that's why I thought she could talk to Valentina and smack some sense into her.

Even though Gianna isn't her mom, she knows who she is, and what she did to her father. Maybe if Bria were to tell her the things she's told me, then Valentina may listen.

Probably not, but it's worth a shot.

"Spit it out."

She knows me well because we're both schemers. She promises she's stopped dealing her dad's shit. But I'm not too sure.

"Remember the girl I was telling you about?"

"How can I forget?" she replies, tongue in cheek.

I ignore her quip. "I can't leave her with Gianna."

"She's a big girl, Lenny. You can't save everyone."

"She isn't everyone," I correct, unable to keep the hostility from my tone. "She's a pain in the ass, but she's my pain in the ass. I have to at least try."

"Try what?" Bria asks, eyeing me suspiciously.

"Maybe you could talk to her."

"About?"

"About fucking unicorns. What do you think?" I reply while she chuckles, humored by my discomfort.

"I don't know why you think me talking to her will change her mind, but sure, I owe you."

"You owe me jack shit," I clarify because she doesn't owe me a thing.

She lets the matter slide. "Just tell me when and how because I don't think Gianna is going to welcome me over for cake and tea."

She's right, which is why I reach for my phone and text Valentina the motel's address and ask her to meet me right now.

"You must really love her."

"Don't use words I don't understand."

She nods, sipping her beer, knowing better than to argue because her battles are yet to come.

When a knock sounds at the door, I take a deep breath because this is either the smartest idea I've ever had or the dumbest.

Bria doesn't stir from reading her book.

Standing, I have three seconds to call this off, but instead, I open the door and see Valentina. She looks at me with curiosity. I knew it would get the better of her and that she'd come.

"So, care to tell me what we're doing in this shithole?"

I hear Bria chuckle from behind. So does Valentina as she stands on her toes to look over my shoulder, eyes narrowed.

I open the door wide, welcoming her in.

She steps inside cautiously, and when she takes in the scene before her, she is clearly confused. Her attention bounces between Lewis and Bria before it stays on Bria. She can guess who the guy passed out in the bed is, but she has no idea who the pink-haired girl reading *Macbeth* is.

"Sit," I order her.

She simply stands and folds her arms.

Well, this is off to a great start…

"That's Lewis, my brother. I found him because Gianna knew where he was this entire time. She also knew he was a junkie but never told me that. I could have helped him before he became that." I point at the bed, angered. "If she actually gave a fuck about anyone other than herself, then she would have told me years ago."

"It's not her fault your brother chose the path he did," Valentina says, not a lick of judgment toward Lewis. For that, I'm glad.

"No, I know that, but it is her fault for purposely holding on to information when I asked her time and time again, and she blatantly lied to my face."

I'm trying so hard not to yell, but just the thought of Gianna has me wanting to stab something.

"Who is she?" Valentina doesn't hide her judgment this time when she glares at Bria.

Bria looks at me because this is my show.

"This is Bria."

"Who is she?" she repeats, not interested in names.

I don't want to give too much away, but how do I expect Valentina to trust me without telling her the truth?

I hope to fuck I don't live to regret this.

"You remember Aldo, the man you said was coming for us? Well, Aldo is Gianna's ex-husband. And this, this is his daughter."

I look at Bria, ensuring this is okay.

She simply nods.

Valentina is utterly still. I don't know if mentioning Aldo has stirred up feelings in her that still plague her dreams, but I need to tell her everything and hope it works.

"Aldo is Gianna's biggest rival, and we know she doesn't like competition. She trained us to take him down because who would suspect two kids?"

"How do you know this?"

But I don't need to answer.

"You traitor, Lenny. You're siding with Aldo after everything Gianna has done for us!"

"Gianna isn't the hero in this story! For fuck's sake! Open your eyes. Look what she did to us! Look at Lewis! I could have helped him before he got to that! And look at what she's turned you into. She's turned you into her!

"She knew where your mother was this entire time, yet she held out all these years to tell you. She is fucking evil! She uses people. She doesn't love. She's taught us that."

Valentina exhales slowly. "You know nothing about my mother. Gianna had her reasons!"

"Such as?" I ask, incredulous to this horseshit.

"She was trying to protect me."

"No, sweetheart, she is trying to *control* you. There's a difference!"

"Lenny," Bria says, trying to calm me down as she stands. "Hi, Valentina. You don't know me, and if I were in your shoes, I would be fucking angry too. But what Lenny says is true. Gianna was married to my dad for years.

"He loved her with all his heart. But the only reason she stayed was to steal from him and turn his men, his world, against him."

Valentina looks seconds away from ripping out Bria's throat. I stand between them, a gesture that doesn't go unnoticed by Valentina.

"I mean you no harm. I only want to help Lenny because I'm the one who dealt drugs to his brother. Lenny could have killed me for what I've done, but he didn't. He cares about people. He cares about you.

"But Gianna doesn't."

Valentina's anger simmers when she hears Bria's confession.

"Please, come with me," I say, hoping she finally sees reason. "I'm not going back there ever again. I understand if you want to stay, but I just…" I can't finish my sentence because the words get stuck in my throat.

"Where will we go?" Valentina asks, walking toward me.

We? Is there a we in this equation, then?

"Aldo will give us a place to stay."

"And what happens to Gianna?"

My silence answers her question.

"Your father was kind to me," Valentina says to Bria, surprising me. "I remember him. He meant everything he said."

Bria nods. "Look, he's a pain in the ass, but he means well."

Valentina's lips twitch.

I don't know what is happening right now, but it's not bad. "Okay."

"Okay?" I ask, confused.

"Okay, I'll come. But I need to get my things. Gianna isn't home. So if we go now, we can—"

I don't let her finish. I wrap her in my arms and hug her tight. I can't believe this actually fucking worked. I look at Bria, nodding in gratitude.

Bria waits downstairs as Valentina packs as much stuff as she can into her overnight bag.

I can't help but continue looking at my watch because time is of the essence. Each second spent here is a second closer to getting caught.

"Look, whatever you need, we'll buy, okay? Let's go." I grab her wrists, stopping her from rifling through her drawers.

But she looks at me with almost sadness. "I know, it's just, this is the first time I've ever owned anything that was mine. It's hard turning your back on something when you've had nothing. I know it's stupid."

I'm such a dumbass. Of course she's nostalgic. This is the only home she's ever known.

"No, it's not stupid. I'm sorry. Take your time."

I let her go, and she smiles, but it's bittersweet. "So, Bria is pretty."

"Is she?"

Valentina rolls her eyes. "Like you didn't notice. It's fine. You like her. I get it."

"Hold up, I like her?" I ask because, what's that got to do with anything?

She turns her back and walks into the walk-in closet. But I follow.

"Can we not do this now?"

"You're the one who's making a big deal about it," she has the gall to reply as she rips a coat down from a hanger.

"No, I'm not the one who brought something so ridiculous up."

"So you don't think she's pretty, then?" she asks, spinning around.

"She's fucking pretty, but so what?" There's no point denying it.

"Have you fucked her?"

"Are you fucking serious right now?"

Her cheeks turn a lovely shade of red. If this were any other time, I would revel in her jealousy. But now, this is just pissing me off.

"So that's a yes, then. But, I mean, who haven't you fucked? She was your brother's drug dealer, for fuck's sake! And now we're going to live with her and her father! And you think here is bad."

Valentina stands her ground, daring me to challenge her. We do not have time for this shit, but fuck me, she needs to be punished for being so goddamned disobedient time and time again.

She doesn't stand a chance as I grab her by the throat and slam her back to the wall. She tries to fight me off, but I only grip her harder.

"I'm not fucking her," I say, slipping a hand under her skirt and rubbing over the front of her underwear. She's wet.

"I don't care who you fuck."

I simply laugh in response.

Her moans are muffled because I've not let her throat go. But she enjoys the pain. I can tell by the way her breaths quicken as I tighten my grip.

"You're a bad liar, sweetheart." I'm not gentle as I sink two fingers into her wet pussy and fuck her with them.

I will never tire of this.

Of the feel of her.

Of the way her breathless whimpers sound.

I'm so hooked on her, regardless of what my aloof actions may convey.

I'm so fucking in love with her and will do anything for her.

I would die for her, which is very probable in our world. I want to choke her most days, but I wouldn't change her in any way because her tenacity and strength to stand up for what she believes in make me love her all the more.

The moment we met was fated in the stars and sealed with a bloodstained kiss.

I watch the way she surrenders to me, the only time she ever does. But I know this is a war she doesn't mind losing because it's one we both win.

"Kiss me," she whispers, her body bending to my will.

I slam my mouth over hers, and we kiss like this is the last day on earth. And in some ways, it may be because a new future awaits.

She moans into my mouth as I fuck her mouth and pussy with a hunger I only ever feel when with Valentina. With two fingers inside her hot pussy, I slide a third finger around to her ass and gently rub over it.

She gasps into my mouth but doesn't shy away.

"Every inch of you is mine," I state against her lips because this isn't up for discussion. "You were mine from the very moment we met. Say it."

This is the only time she's happy to concede.

"I'm yours, Lennon. Always and forever. No matter what."

No matter what? Why does that sound as though there is finality to her tone?

She kisses me longingly, lowering her guard.

Her body is lax. Her breathless whimpers filled with desire. With two fingers still inside her, I rub over her clit and watch with utter craving as she comes to my touch. She doesn't close her eyes. She looks into mine, allowing me to see a vulnerability that is so beautiful.

"I want you inside me."

She tugs at my belt and unfastens my jeans. My cock is hard. Her wish is my command.

Spinning her around, I lift her skirt and admire her glorious ass. There is only one response to seeing something of utter perfection.

I slap it.

She moans, arching her back, offering it to me.

So I smack it again, harder this time.

And again.

Her ass cheeks are pink, remnants of my handprint lingering on her supple flesh.

Gripping her hips, I enter her pussy swiftly, and the moment I hit deep, I don't move, allowing her to feel every inch of me.

She feels like a hot, wet kiss on my cock. I need to fuck her, and I need it to be rough. She wiggles that ass, an invitation to give in to my desires and gorge myself until I'm stuffed full.

There is nothing gentle about this, and the louder she moans, the harder I fuck. Her hands are splayed against the wall, using it as support because I do not give her a reprieve. Using her hips as leverage, I bounce her back onto my cock, engrossed in the way her ass looks as I'm fucking her into a legless stupor.

She spreads her legs, taking me deeper.

Bending down, I bite her neck, wanting to tear her apart.

I watch as she blindly feels her way toward a shelf, and when she produces a flick knife, I only fuck her harder.

She passes me the knife behind her back.

I know what she wants.

Blood has always been our triggers, and there's nothing more carnal than bloodletting.

Still embedded deep inside her, I slice between her neck and shoulder and take her flesh into my mouth. With a sharp pull, I lick away the metallic sting, sending every nerve ending in my body into a frenzy.

She moans, dropping her shoulder, offering me more.

And more I take.

I fuck her without mercy as I suck at her wound, and when I reach around to play with her clit, she comes with a loud cry. She shifts so I slip out of her, only to turn around, yank the knife from my hand, and slash it across my chest.

She bends low and frantically sucks at the wound, peering at me with those trusting eyes.

I cup her head to my chest, feeding her my blood. It does something to me. Offering your life source to your beloved is a new form of obsession, and I'm so fucking hooked.

I lift her and slam her back onto my cock as she wraps her legs around my waist.

I fuck her, eyes locked as she makes another incision across my throat and sucks.

Our mouths are coated in blood.

Our bodies entwine in a beautiful union.

She pulls away and presses her mouth to mine.

Our bodies are one.

I can't help but come with a sated moan.

Valentina rocks against me as if wishing to milk every last drop out of me.

I'm lost to her, to this moment, but when she meets my eyes, I realize this was all a ruse to bide time. And when I hear a scream downstairs, I realize that the look I see reflected in her eyes is…guilt.

"What have you done?"

Before she has a chance to reply, the door bursts open. I quickly turn my back to protect her, but when I'm sucker punched in the stomach, it seems she isn't the one needing protection.

I've not seen this asshole before, but no doubt, he's Gianna's new lapdog. When he goes to punch me again, I duck and slam my fist into his jaw. His head snaps back, and I'm on him, knocking us both to the floor.

Anger courses through me because, right now, my mindset is attack first, ask questions later.

Valentina screams, which has me losing concentration for a split second—rookie move on my behalf because ten billion volts of electricity run through my body, leaving me gasping for air.

A fucking Taser.

I will my body to stop being a little bitch, but it's no use when he tases me again before I succumb to the screams of Valentina.

I wake with no recollection of who I am.

Where I'm at.

It's a nice feeling to escape who I was. I figure I'm not a good guy as I'm hanging from chains on a basement wall.

I tug at the metal cuffs, but it's no use. I'm not going anywhere soon.

"Have a nice nap, Sleeping Beauty?"

Turning to my left, I see pink hair…

I'm then sucked into a whirlwind of color before I'm spat back out into this reality that can suck my dick.

"Where the fuck is she?"

I don't need to clarify who.

"I had no other choice," the star of the show says.

Gianna steps out from the shadows, and if I wasn't chained to a wall, this would be fucking comical. But right now, I'm far from laughing.

"You had a dozen other choices," I correct, not interested in playing her games. "Where's Valentina?"

She's not down here, imprisoned. So where is she?

Gianna examines her red nails as if bored to be here. "She is where she should be."

"What the fuck is that supposed to mean?"

"It means she knows what loyalty is. You, however, have chosen your side." Gianna turns her attention to Bria. "You should have minded your own business, *carissima*."

"Yeah, I guess the same could be said about you," Bria replies, unmoved. "My father is going to fucking kill you when he finds out what you've done."

"What I've done?" Gianna says, placing a hand over her heart, faking hurt. "All I'm doing is protecting myself. What anyone would do."

I roll my eyes. "Oh, cut the bullshit. I'm so sick of your lies. We all know how this ends, so let's get a move on, shall we?"

Gianna chuckles.

She is without a doubt enjoying this, and why wouldn't she? She's finally got me by the balls.

"Your father is trying to ruin me. And I cannot have that." Gianna stands perfectly still, which concerns me because she is calculating something. I just don't know what.

"He is only taking back what is rightly his," Bria bites back, defending her dad. "You're the traitor here, not him. You're just upset he's better at it than you are."

I can't hold back my smile because even chained, Bria's smart mouth continues to run.

Gianna, however, doesn't appreciate her sass.

She gestures with her head for her goon to show Bria what happens when one doesn't bend to her will.

The asshole slaps Bria across the cheek. Her head snaps to the side with a loud crack. But she recovers, spitting her spilled blood into his face before a slow grin spreads from cheek to cheek.

He goes to slap her again, but Gianna raises her hand. "Enough."

I doubt she's had a change of heart because she doesn't have one after all. So I wonder what trick she has up her sleeve. And when I hear someone coming down the stairs, I know this is no magic trick.

This is real life.

Valentina appears from the darkness, the horror clear on her face. It makes me feel remotely better that she's not involved in Gianna's devious plans. But that's not entirely true.

I remember how she didn't appear surprised when we were under attack. No doubt she was the one who tipped Gianna off. Was she stalling the whole time?

Disgust suddenly fills my belly, and it shows on my face.

"Don't hate me," Valentina says, reading my thoughts.

I can't look at her right now because I'll say something I'll probably regret. I don't pretend to understand her loyalty to Gianna. But I realize there is nothing I can do to change her mind, which means we will always be on opposing teams.

Regardless of my feelings for her, I know that she and I will never work. So where does that leave us?

Me chained to a wall, it seems.

"Let Bria go. She's got nothing to do with this. I won't fight you."

"We both know that isn't true," Gianna says with a smirk. "That's why you're here. If only you just left well enough alone. But now, you've left me with no other choice."

I'm so done with this bitch.

"Oh, blah, blah, fucking blah. Go on then, let's do this."

"Lenny…" Valentina gasps, understanding this is a fight until one of us is dead. And seeing as I'm the one chained to the wall, the odds are not in my favor.

"Mario." Just his name is enough of a cue for this motherfucker to jump to command, like the good dog that he is.

Mario punches me in the stomach, and as my head drops forward, he punches me in the jaw.

"Oh, you're a big fucking tough guy," I quip, laughter erupting from me. "You're just another one of Gianna's little bitches. Fucking pussy."

Mario doesn't appreciate the constructive criticism and kicks me in the ribs. He cracks two.

"Stop it!" Valentina screams, rushing forward and latching onto Mario's wrist to stop him from punching me again.

But I don't want her help.

"You chose your side, darling. Own it." And only then do I meet her tormented gaze.

"This was never part of the deal!" she screams, pleading with an unmoved Gianna.

"What deal?" I wheeze, trying to see straight after Mario punches me in the face, breaking my nose.

Valentina's bottom lip trembles.

"What fucking deal?" I scream, not at all moved by Valentina's sudden regret.

"I was to bring her Aldo's daughter, and my mother is free," she confesses, head bowed.

Fuck you, universe, and your sick sense of humor. I

practically delivered Bria to her on a silver fucking platter. I thought I was doing something to help Valentina. But I've done the complete fucking opposite.

"You do realize she doesn't want Bria to catch up on old times! She's going to use her as collateral! Aldo will do whatever she wants because unlike her, he actually has a heart! Fuck, Valentina!"

"I'm sorry," she whispers, her regret clear. "I didn't think she would hurt you."

"Does that make it any better?" I demand, shaking my head at her. "You're okay with someone who has nothing to fucking do with this being chained to a wall because Gianna has to play dirty? I don't know who you are anymore."

She gasps, wounded by my words.

"And I don't plan on hurting him," Gianna says calmly. "But Bria isn't so innocent. What would your father think if he knew you were stealing from him?"

I don't know how Gianna knows, but this isn't good.

Bria doesn't waver, however. "I'm dead anyway, aren't I? So what difference does it make?"

Gianna walks forward and strokes Bria's cheek with the back of her hand. "You're much more valuable to me alive than you are dead. But I think we need to scare your father a little. What do you think?"

Again, she isn't asking because there isn't a choice.

Mario punches Bria in the stomach. She buckles in half, wheezing for air. Whatever air she manages to get is in vain because he punches her in the face, and the back of her head slams against the concrete wall.

He's about to punch her again but stops when I burst into maniacal laughter.

Hardly the appropriate response, considering our circumstances, but the line between sanity and going fucking mad blurred long ago.

"What are you laughing about?" Mario asks, appearing genuinely offended, which just makes me laugh harder.

Once I catch my breath, I reply, "You realize you sound like a little bitch when you punch, right?"

In case he doesn't, I mimic a sound akin to a dying hyena.

"Must exert a lot of energy to hit a defenseless girl."

Mario doesn't appreciate the jab and shows me this by punching me in the stomach. Then the face. He busts open my lip. And it's exactly what I was hoping for.

Just as he's about to hit me again, Gianna stops him.

"Your services are no longer needed, Mario. You may go."

He looks at her like she's spoken in another language. But he eventually gets the hint and leaves.

When we're alone, Gianna smirks, looking at me in anger or awe. I can't decide which.

"Very clever," she says, folding her arms across her chest.

"Baiting him so he hits you instead of Bria. But your chivalry will get the better of you. Once again, your humanity is your downfall."

"Listen to yourself! My humanity? I'm not a fucking robot! But I don't expect someone like you to understand. No wonder you're alone; no one could ever love a heartless bitch like you."

The room falls silent.

I've struck a nerve. I can see it in Gianna's face.

Usually, she's expressionless, but this one stung.

"What's wrong, darling? The truth hurt?"

It's apparent on her face that she's weighing over what to do next. Usually, she wouldn't react. But this time is different.

She walks over to Bria and does something which surprises me—she unlocks the chains from around her wrists. Bria is confused as she shakes out her hands. The fact I'm still chained, however, has me guessing my words are about to come back and bite me in the ass.

"Clean his face," she orders Bria, offering her a handkerchief.

Bria looks at Gianna like this is some sort of trick, but when she sees she is in fact serious, she takes the handkerchief and walks to me. Her back is turned to Gianna, so she speaks to me with her eyes.

She too is wondering what the fuck is going on.

She begins cleaning the blood from my face carefully, her eyes never leaving mine. She is the one who is free. Therefore, she is the one who needs to fight. And I make that clear as I look over her shoulder at Gianna and then back to her.

She nods subtly, understanding.

"I don't know what it is about you, Lenny, that has women wanting to care for you."

"I don't expect someone like you to understand, Gianna, seeing as you're alone because no one can stand being around you."

Bria's lips twitch.

"This upsets you, doesn't it?" she asks Valentina who I have purposely ignored.

"Yes. What are you doing?"

"I want you to see men for who they really are. Men will give you attention until something better comes along. They're all the same. The sooner you see that, it'll save you a lifetime of pain. Why did you do that for Bria?"

"Because I was the one who got her into this mess." I look at Bria, who shakes her head. She makes it clear she doesn't want an apology.

"Men are also liars," Gianna says to Valentina. "You like Bria. There's nothing wrong with that."

Bria's cheeks blister red.

I'm damned if I do, and I'm damned if I don't. I refute; I hurt Bria's feelings. I don't say a word; I hurt Valentina's feelings.

I soon understand Gianna's game plan.

"And she likes you."

"If you're trying to make a point, get to it," I say, not interested in playing this game.

"Kiss him then and prove me wrong."

Bria looks at me, desperate I tell her what to do. We both know Gianna isn't going to let this slide.

It's just a kiss, right? What harm can it do? Other than hurt Valentina, that is, which is why Bria leans forward and presses her lips to mine.

It feels foreign to have someone's lips on mine other than Valentina's. It's over quicker than it began. But Gianna tsks us.

"You can do better than that."

I know she won't stop until she makes her point. So I nod at Bria, hinting it's best to get this over with as quickly as possible.

Bria takes a breath before slamming her lips to mine. She kisses me with passion, and it's evident none of this is staged. She feels something for me, just as Gianna said. She wraps her hand around my nape and deepens the kiss.

I kiss her back, hating what this is doing to Valentina, but this is what she wanted. She sided with Gianna. This is now the consequence of her choices.

Bria is in control because I'm chained, but I'm a willing participant. A part of me, the asshole part, is pleased to know I'm hurting Valentina. It's a side of myself I'm not proud of. But goddamn, it feels good.

Bria moans into my mouth, biting my bottom lip before sucking it softly.

"Bravo," Gianna says, victory loaded. "But I still think we can do better."

Bria places one final kiss on my mouth before pulling away. She only seems to realize the dangerous door we just opened.

"Fuck you," she says, turning over her shoulder and glaring at Gianna.

I lock eyes with Valentina, and any part of me which relished hurting her is soon squashed because I realize she will never look at me the same way ever again.

It seems we only ever hurt ourselves and will continue to do so for the rest of our lives. We are toxic, but like most things that want to kill you, they're the things that make you feel most alive.

"Touch him," Gianna orders as Valentina closes her eyes tight.

"What? No," Bria gasps, shaking her head.

But again, we don't have a choice.

"Okay, fine. If you won't, then Mario will. Mario!"

"All right!" Bria cries, tears in her eyes.

Gianna won't be satisfied until she humiliates us all.

Bria strokes my face with an unfamiliar touch. I compare it to Valentina's. My body doesn't respond because it's not Bria's touch it craves.

Gianna clears her throat, hinting to continue.

"Just do it," I say under my breath, giving her permission.

"I'm sorry," she mouths, but she has nothing to be sorry for.

She touches my chest and down to my stomach. Her touch is apprehensive. But she continues. When she gets to my belt, she works her hands back up, but Gianna stops her.

"Don't be coy. We're all friends here."

Bria exhales heavily before moving her hands over the front of my pants. She quickly works her way back up, but Gianna storms over and grips her wrist.

"You are really testing my patience!" She coaxes Bria to touch my cock, ensuring she never breaks eye contact with me.

I do the same because I want Gianna to know she'll never win. She can break my body, but she will never break my spirit. As long as I have air in my lungs, I'll never stop hunting her. So let her have her fun because the moment I'm released, she's free game.

"You're nothing but a warm body for men, Valentina. Let this be a lesson learned."

"You and your fucking lessons can go to hell," I spit, refusing to buckle.

But I can feel my dick beginning to stir.

Gianna is still in charge, using Bria's hand as merely a tool as she continues rubbing over the front of my pants. She realizes she won't get the results she wants this way. So she unfastens my belt and undoes my jeans. When she places Bria's hand down my pants and forces her to rub over my cock, I envision the many ways I plan on killing her.

The thought of restraining her and placing a plastic bag over her head to limit her air supply, only to liberate her lungs by giving her false hope that she will survive, is what gets me hard. I imagine peeling the skin from her body with precision so that she's still alive, just a meat suit for the scavengers to eat her flesh while I stand by and watch her die a slow, painful death, sipping a neat scotch.

The thoughts of torturing her in the most creative ways have my cock swelling. I wish I had control over it, but this is what usually happens when someone rubs over a guy's cock. We aren't usually that composed when it comes to our dicks. And for me, blood and sex always seem to go hand in hand.

Gianna of course assumes I'm hard because of what she's doing, but little does she know I'm turned on by knowing that I'm the one who will end her fucking life. I don't know when or how. But what I do know is that one day I will have the satisfaction of being the last face she sees as I fucking choke the life from her.

"See, *piccola*, they're just animals in the end. They don't care about anyone other than themselves."

"That may be the case for you because no man could ever love you."

Gianna's face turns a lovely shade of red. She's mad. "So your dick isn't hard then by another woman's hand?"

I look at Valentina, who looks at me with nothing but hatred. "Don't say I didn't warn you. You wanted this. What did you think was going to happen?"

"I didn't expect I would be watching two women jerking you off!" she exclaims, storming over. "Enough. You've made your point."

"No, I haven't because you're angry, and that means you still care," Gianna refutes, forcing Bria to move her hand faster. "You can stop this."

"How?" Valentina screams, and I hate that Gianna has this effect on her. But I cannot continue begging her to see the truth.

"We are at the top of the food chain," Gianna explains while Bria struggles to shrug Gianna off. It's fruitless. "We take what we want because we are the predators. Everyone else is nothing but merely prey. What do you want?"

I clench my teeth and fight the urge to come. Just because my dick is hard, doesn't mean I want to come.

Valentina takes a deep breath. She looks at Bria like she wants to rip her head off.

"No, don't."

But that's probably the worst thing I could say because it only adds fuel to this out-of-control fire.

Valentina doesn't hesitate as she grabs the back of Bria's

neck and drags her off me. Bria fights, but Valentina is trained to defend herself, so she doesn't stand a chance. She slams Bria's face into the brick wall, instantly breaking her nose.

"Valentina!" I scream, needing her to see reason and stop this.

My hard-on is long gone as I'm appalled by what I see.

Gianna finally keeps her hands to herself, watching the mayhem she caused erupt before her with nothing but a smile. I yank at my chains, snarling like the feral animal I am.

"Best you kill me now because I promise you, I won't fucking stop until you're dead."

Gianna laughs, humored. "You can try, but you will always fail because I own the one thing that means anything to you."

Her comment infuriates me, and I lunge forward, the chains the only thing protecting her from my fury. "You don't own her."

"You know that's not true." She steps forward, standing on her toes as she whispers into my ear, "If it were, I wouldn't be able to control her the way I can."

I don't think twice as I connect with her forehead, headbutting her.

Her arrogance gets the better of her as I catch her off guard. She stumbles backward, stunned. I lunge forward, the chains rattling, restricting me from ripping off her head and fucking the wound.

"Valentina, you are no better than her if you don't stop this!"

But she doesn't listen.

She drags Bria by the hair and lifts her, slamming her back against the wall as she restrains her once again. I guess it's a small miracle she didn't kill her.

I look at Valentina, wondering where the innocent girl I once knew has gone because the person I see now is a replica of the monster who raised us.

She walks over to me and cups my chin between two fingers. There is nothing heartfelt about the touch.

"You make me sick."

I grin in response. "The feeling is more than mutual, sweetheart."

And I mean every single word.

I hate and love her all in the same breath.

Gianna has finally won; Valentina and I are on opposing teams, and I wonder who will win.

She slaps my cheek before leaving me for good.

CHAPTER 16

VALENTINA

've scrubbed my skin raw, yet I still feel so dirty.

What the fuck have I done?

I stand under the shower spray, and the water is so hot, it feels like my skin is peeling. But the pain is a reminder that I'm alive.

I fucked up.

But I didn't think Gianna would harm Lenny. I gave her Bria on the proviso that Lenny was to remain unharmed. But she lied.

I thought it would finally be over and that my mom could

live the life she deserved with Aldo paying for his sins. But all I did was make things so much worse.

I don't know how to make this better.

I could go to Aldo and tell him what I did and perhaps strike a deal with him. But if I do that, I know I'm dead. He won't forgive me. Look at what he did to my mom.

The one person I would go to for advice is chained in the basement, and it's all my fault.

I need to make this right, but images of him responding to Bria's touch have tears burning my eyes. I don't know what to do.

I don't understand why I have such loyalty to Gianna and my mother—neither woman cares about me. Look what they've done to me. The only person who cared now hates my guts, and he has every right to.

I lower my chin, the water cascading around me, drowning out the voices in my head. I'm so fucked up. I wish I wasn't, but I'm damaged goods, and I don't know how to fix it.

But perhaps that's where I've gone wrong.

I don't think I can ever be "fixed." I doubt I'll ever be normal, and I realize I like Lenny because he is busted up inside like me. We are two halves of the same broken heart.

And the only way to repair that heart is to rip out the heart of the monster who created you.

This has been a long time coming, and I guess I was biding

my time, waiting for the right moment. But there will never be a right time to kill the motherfucker who destroyed your innocence because he deserves to die a thousand deaths.

But alas, humanity doesn't allow it.

So I'll just have to make sure the one death is as painful as a lifetime of torture.

Switching off the water, I'm on autopilot as I dry off and hunt through my drawers for what to wear.

A white nightgown.

I plait my hair into two pigtails just like he used to. Tonight is about being reborn, and what better way to welcome my arrival into the world than by ending the life of the asshole who stole mine.

I slip into my combat boots and slide my knife snugly inside.

When I look at my appearance in the mirror, a sense of happiness fills me. Most girls would be gushing over what's in fashion, but not me. I only feel any shred of emotion when bloodshed is looming.

I've accepted that I'm beyond fucked up, and the only way to deal with it is to give in to my temptations, not fight them. Fighting is fruitless. This is who I am. Who I was always destined to become.

I sneak out of my bedroom, ignoring the pang of regret I have for leaving Lenny behind. But he made his choice. We will never be on the same side. We may love one another, but our determination and individual needs will always stand in the way of us ever living side by side in harmony.

My only love sprang from my only hate...

I don't know what that means for us, but I realize I can only ever rely on myself.

Trusting others only ever gets you hurt. Or forces you to watch the boy you love getting felt up by two other women.

Looks like he made good on his word as I remember what he said.

"If you don't say it, I'll make you watch me fuck someone else, tesoro mio."

The memories only incite this inner rage, and I jump into my car, taking off into the dark night where I'm one with the shadows, just how I've always been.

I'm a robot behind the wheel.

My mind is clear.

I wish I could say I was hit with an epiphany, and I uncovered all of life's mysteries. That I saw the light, and I was saved.

I wish for so many things, but there's no fighting biology.

Or fate.

I was born a killer.

Fighting my nature is a battle I'll always lose.

And I'm sick of trying to be good because when I pull up by St. Maria's Orphanage, there's apparently no good inside me.

There never was.

The mask I wore has been ripped away, and this is my true face—the face of a killer.

And now, the only thing I can do is embrace the real me.

I don't bother concealing my car. I don't care if he knows I'm approaching. I think he always knew this day would come.

My boots sound softly against the pavement, the only noise filling the still night. It feels as though nothing living inhabits the surroundings because things only come to St. Maria's to wither and decay until all that's left is a shell of what once was.

Closing my eyes, I extend my hand and brush my fingers against the tall chain-linked fence. Memories assault me of when I was trapped on the other side, wishing I was able to break free.

However, now that I'm on this side, I realize that freedom isn't what it's cut out to be. I'm as much a prisoner on the outside as I was on the inside. And that's because I'm a prisoner within myself.

Counting in my head, I stop at fifty-seven. It's here where I find the same small hole in the fence. I used to stare at it, mesmerized by the possibilities of this exit I could take. I could run away and never be found.

But where would I go?

No one wanted me. Not even my own mother.

Which is why I don't understand why I have this sense of

loyalty to her. Perhaps I have a heart after all.

Scoffing at that notion, I open my eyes and bend low to crawl through the hole. Thick flowering bushes hide it but no longer flourish as nothing grows on this barren land. I slip through with ease and keep to the shadows as I make my way through the open field.

I remember first laying eyes on Lenny as he rescued Cat. How that event changed my life forevermore. When I approach the spot where he once stood, I peer upward at the room that was once mine.

The attic.

Locked away from the world because I was unlovable.

My fingernails dig into my palms as I curl them into fists because, how can I love when I was only ever shown hate?

Sniffing away my tears, I continue my journey into the past that I need to slaughter to embrace whatever future I have. The doors are locked, but that doesn't stop me as I retrieve my knife to pick it.

It pops open with ease.

It's eerily silent when I step inside.

Memories overwhelm me, and I close my eyes, allowing my equilibrium to settle. I refuse to be a victim to them.

Reopening my eyes, I see nothing but revenge as I stroll down the hallway. I peer into the rooms of fellow orphans like I once was. I wonder if Father Merry has taken an interest in one in particular as he did with me.

This only fuels my need to do the most unspeakable things to him and do so with a smile.

It's after ten, so he will be in the chapel, saying a prayer. I know this because once he made peace with God, he would come to me and drag me to the depths of hell where he violated my soul, assuring I would never be accepted into the pearly white gates of Heaven.

He ensured I was to forever be sullied.

A whore.

A sinner.

Father Merry isn't the reason I'm this way. I was born this way. But he played a part in shaping who I became...and now, it's time I give grace because I embrace this woman I am with both hands.

This is who I am.

And this is the only thing I know.

Opening the door quietly, I see Father Merry kneeling behind a pew, his hands interlaced. The only light is from the candles burning softly on the altar. I make sure to lock the door behind me.

What a stage it will set.

Father Merry isn't aware of my presence; I have Gianna to thank for that. She taught me well. Muted whispers pass through those sinful lips, lips which lied. Lips that defiled me in ways that are most despicable.

It only seems fair I return the favor.

Silver rosary beads are intertwined through his fingers, fingers that violated parts of me that left me incapacitated for days.

"No, please stop, it hurts."

"Hush, child, you are a vessel of the Lord."

The feeble voice of that scared child is foreign. I don't know who she is any longer. All that remains is a vacant husk who knows nothing but pain.

Father Merry's fingers cease from sliding over each rosary bead.

He knows I'm here.

"I always knew you'd be back," he says, his back still turned. "A sinner always comes home. Pray with me."

His voice is calm.

I do as he says and round the pew, coming face-to-face with the monsters in my dreams.

He hasn't changed.

He still resembles a kind man with his blue eyes and blond hair. A cleft chin and silver glasses. He looks like a man here to save those who have sinned. But he is the most dangerous monster of all. The unsuspecting are the ones who lure those in with their smile and charm, as one is unaware of the demons they harbor and the fear they will instill in their hearts.

He doesn't meet my eyes.

He bends his head and continues to pray.

I kneel beside him and interlace my hands. I can't remember the last time I prayed.

Our Father…

I didn't know how I'd feel being here again. Yes, the memories are rampant, but there is a clarity I've never felt before. I wait for Father Merry to finish his prayer because they're to be his last.

"So you're here to kill me like the sinner I knew you were?"

I'll give it to him; even in the face of death, he isn't afraid. I would admire that trait if it didn't belong to my abuser.

"You're right, Father Merry," I reply, eyes focused ahead. "I'm a sinner. I always have been. But unlike you, I don't hide behind a veil of falseness. I embrace who I am. I embrace the woman you created."

"Do not blame your immorality on me. I looked after you when no one else did."

"You looked after yourself," I clarify without faltering. "You don't remember all the times you came to me and told me to be quiet as you did God's work? You don't remember all the times you forced me to my knees so I could gag on your filthy cock?

"Because I remember. I cannot forget. You ensured you remained with me long after you were gone, for what you did was an act so heinous that I could never forget it. But that's what you wanted, is it not? For me to always remember you."

I finally turn and lock eyes with Father Merry, who was my boogeyman for as long as I can remember. But now, he doesn't look that scary.

"You are a whore, just like Mary Magdalene." He crosses himself as if that can absolve him of his sins.

A laugh bubbles from my throat, and Father Merry cocks a brow.

"Whatever are you laughing at?"

His stuffiness just has me laughing harder.

"You. I can't believe I was afraid of you for so long. You're pathetic."

And he is.

I once thought him to be some magical being, him the puppeteer and me the puppet. But now I see him for what he really is. The monster I feared is nothing but a coward. A pathetic little man made up of nothing but flesh and bone.

Flesh and bone, which I intend to peel from his body until nothing is left.

Ashes to ashes.

Dust to dust.

"Say your prayers, Father. Make peace with your God."

Father Merry nods and returns his gaze to the altar, mumbling the word of the Lord under his breath.

Excitement courses through me because I have been waiting for this day for what seems like a lifetime. I don't know if this will help me heal, but it sure as shit will feel good.

However, it seems this asshole won't go down without a fight.

Father Merry reaches for a Bible and catches me unawares as he whacks me in the face with it. Instantly, blood pours from my nose. He launches from the seat and runs down the aisle toward the door.

The thrill of the chase only fuels the hunter within, so I do what any predator does.

As I take off, blood spills into my mouth, and the familiar metallic tang feeds the beast, which is forever hungry for violence and carnage. Mid-run, I reach for the knife in my boot and throw it with precision.

I never miss.

Father Merry drops to the floor with the knife embedded in his leg. He howls in pain while I roll my eyes.

"Oh, stop being such a baby. It's just a scratch."

He's crawling on his belly toward the door, his hand outstretched, freedom within reach. The sight pleases me immensely.

I stand in front of him, blocking his path. He tries to get up, but I stomp on his fingers, breaking two. His wails grow louder. As does the need to inflict lots of pain.

"You won't get away with this! Help!"

"Your God can't help you, Father. He can't hear your cries.

Just like He couldn't hear mine."

Memories of Father Merry's hand over my mouth as he mounted me from behind assault me. I remember the way he tore at me, not caring about the damage he was doing to me mentally and physically.

Dropping to a knee, I yank the knife from his leg and kick him in the ribs. He rolls onto his back, attempting to stand, but I bend low and violently stretch out his arm, stabbing the blade through the middle of his palm and impaling him to the floor.

He tries to pry himself free, but it only results in the knife cutting in deeper.

"Take what you want. Just let me go!"

In response, I spit in his face. It's colored with my blood. "I can't believe I actually once feared you. You're fucking pathetic. Nothing but a scared little coward."

"Please."

"Please?" I mock, gripping his throat and thrusting his head back at a painful angle. "You're begging me to show mercy?"

His eyes plead for me to let him go.

"Where was my compassion when you gave me to those men like I was nothing but a toy? Where was my mercy when you raped me over and over again? And what about the other boys and girls you tortured? Where was their compassion, Father Merry? Where?" I scream, punching him in the face when he tries to answer.

Blood pours from his nose, which I just broke.

I rip off his clerical collar because he is a disgrace to God. However, this is one souvenir I wish to keep as I place it into my boot for safekeeping.

I'm done playing.

Yanking out the knife, I swiftly pull back on his arm, dislocating it.

He inhales, his mouth opening and closing as sound is replaced with pain. I yank him up and drag him to the altar. He tries to fight, so I punch him in the stomach, winding him. He's wounded, his arm hanging useless as he drags his leg.

The trail of blood he leaves behind is a visual that is nothing but beautiful.

I force him to bend over the altar. Once again, he tries to fight, so I thrust my knife into his uninjured hand, impaling him. He is buckled, unable to bear weight on his wounded leg. But he is forced to stay upright.

Looking at the pillar candle on the altar, I have a wonderful idea.

Yanking down his trousers, I grab the candle and don't give him a chance to beg or brace for what comes as I ram the lit end straight into his ass.

He cries raucously. Blood coats the white candle.

Leaning over his shoulder, I whisper into his ear as I force the candle deeper into his channel, "Hurts, doesn't it?"

I begin to fuck him with it, just as crudely as he did to me. I push it so deep inside him that it robs him of air. Only to retract it so I can shove it back in deeper.

"P-please," he begs, a pathetic heap as I defile him. "Please stop."

"What was that, Father?" I ask, placing my ear inches from his lips. "You want me to stop?"

"Yes, child. Please. You win."

I tsk him. "There aren't any winners, Father Merry. Only victims created by your hand."

Pulling out the candle, I toss it on the floor.

He sighs in relief.

I step back and look at my handiwork.

He's a bleeding mess, but it still isn't enough. It never will be.

Peering up at the large wooden crucifix on a stand behind the altar, I wonder if perhaps God has spoken because I'm about to outdo myself.

Father Merry sags as I pull out the knife from his hand. I grab him by the back of the neck and shove him.

"Say the Lord's Prayer," I order just as he once did to me.

He's defeated. He doesn't fight as I strip him naked. The gold crucifix he wears around his neck brings back memories of when he lay on top of me, it swaying before my eyes as he buried himself deep inside me.

I yank it off, wanting to destroy it with the man who wears it.

Kicking down the crucifix, I lay it on the carpet. Father Merry has gone to his happy place, but fuck no. He doesn't get such clemency.

I slap his cheek, awakening him to the reality of what's to come. He continues to recite the Lord's Prayer in hopes that some miracle might occur and he will be saved.

"We're past saving. It's time to pay for your sins. Confess your sins, Father. Perhaps the Lord will forgive you and accept you into His kingdom."

"You're nothing but a whore," he pants, his head lolling to the side as spittle runs down his chin. "Just like your mother."

I wish I could prolong this, but I know soon, someone will come looking for him. And besides, he has robbed enough air as it is.

I begin punching every part of him. He doesn't stand a chance. I was born for this, raised to fight. He was always going to lose.

He drops to the floor, and I drag him toward the crucifix. He tries a last-ditch attempt to flee, but I press my boot into his stomach, pinning his back to the wood. Bending down, I yank out his arm and stab my knife into his palm, spearing him to one side of the crucifix.

He turns his neck to look at the knife, understanding how

his life will end. "No."

"Oh yes," I correct with a smile. "You always thought yourself to be God, so it seems fitting you die with your beloved Lord close by."

Thinking on my feet, I reach for a smaller gold crucifix off the altar and drive the pointy end into his other hand, crucifying him.

I position his feet so they can rest on the small ledge underneath the Lord's feet and move the crucifix back to standing behind the altar.

Oh, what a sight this is for all to see—Father Merry naked, bleeding, and crucified.

There is a statue of some saint, arm high as he raises a spear into the air. I pry it from his hand and walk over to Father Merry, whose chin droops to his chest.

I commit this to memory because this memory will now replace the others. I will no longer allow the abuse I suffered to rule me because this now replaces the pain I once felt.

Slapping him awake, I peer into his eyes as I stab the spear into his chest and cut downward. "Ring around the rosie," I sing, severing through flesh and muscle.

The nursery rhyme he sang to me as if to make what he was doing to me okay.

I continue singing as I cut Father Merry from sternum to groin. I pry open the wound and reach inside, disemboweling him.

I would cut out his heart, but I want him alive.

"We all fall down." The song is done. As is Father Merry. "I'll see you in Hell."

Stepping back, I admire my work and tip my face to the heavens.

I've been reborn.

The moment Father Merry stops breathing is when I leave. But not before I wipe my thumb down my forehead and over my eye, leaving a bloody slash to commemorate what was done tonight.

It reminds me of Lenny. How I wish he were here.

I know what I have to do. I have to make things right.

Opening the chapel door, I waltz down the hallway, whistling, uncaring that the sisters scream in horror because I sure as shit probably look a fright in my blood-splattered nightgown.

I know this is the beginning of the end...but I just don't care.

And perhaps I never did.

CHAPTER 17

LENNY

t's quiet, which worries me.

Nothing good ever comes from silence.

Bria won't look at me.

The air is thick with hostility.

It's everything Gianna wanted.

She wanted chaos. She wanted to drive a wedge between us all. And I hate to admit she's succeeded.

I have no idea where Valentina is.

A small part of me thought that perhaps we would prevail and Gianna would lose. But that's not the case. With Bria bound, Gianna has the upper hand, and without a doubt, Aldo will do anything to save his daughter.

And what about Lewis? He will be awake and looking for his next fix. I found him, only to lose him once again. But most likely for good this time.

"Stop thinking so loud," Bria quips, breaking the silence.

"Are you all right?"

She peers at the chains around her wrists.

"Yeah, good point. That was a stupid question." I sigh.

"My father will be here soon."

I nod because she's right.

Gianna has the home-ground advantage. She won't meet Aldo anywhere but here because she knows the moment she steps out of this house, she's dead. That's why she wanted Bria here.

And I delivered her on a silver fucking platter.

"Any ideas?" she asks, reading my thoughts on how screwed we are.

"Apart from ripping out Gianna's heart and feeding it to her?"

Bria's mouth twitches.

"I'm so fucking sorry I involved you in this mess."

"Don't go soft on me now, pretty boy. We both know Gianna always gets what she wants. We'll figure something out. I know my dad, and although he'll come alone and unarmed, his men will be waiting. He'd rather burn down this house with us inside than allow Gianna to win."

She's right.

"I always knew this would end in bloodshed. I just thought—" But I stop because I don't want to be insensitive by adding I always thought Valentina and I would be fighting side by side. Not against each other.

"Even still, you love her." It's not a question but rather a statement, and there's no point denying it because it's true.

I will always choose her. She is my first and last choice because I love her so fucking much. I'll never stop because she is a part of me. And she always will be. But that doesn't mean I won't kill her before she kills me because I know she's out for blood.

Bria's face falls, but her poker face soon slips into place. I wish I could say something that wouldn't sound so fucking lame, but she knows, regardless of what Valentina has done, I will kill anyone who tries to hurt her.

What a fucking simp I've become.

"You're loyal, Lenny, but can you say the same about her?"

"It doesn't matter," I reply because my loyalty will always lie with her.

"We are in this situation because of her! It matters a lot! For fuck's sake."

She has every right to be mad.

Fuck, I'm mad at myself for not being angrier at Valentina for what she's done. But would I have done the same if I were in her shoes? The answer is yes. She is loyal to Gianna, and although we don't agree on that loyalty, I admire her for sticking to her beliefs.

One day, she will see Gianna for what she is, but until that day, I can't give up on trying.

Now is not that day, however, because when I hear the sound of heels stabbing at the stairs, I know the time has come. Gianna saunters down the stairs, her confidence suffocating, and why wouldn't it be? Aldo follows her, at her mercy.

The moment we lock eyes, I know that either he or Gianna will be dead by the end of the night. However, it's apparent that he doesn't know who it will be.

He doesn't cower or show fear. His pride wouldn't allow it. Even though he is the underdog, he won't beg. His relief is clear when he sees that Bria is okay.

"You were always one for theatrics, Gianna," he says, unmoved.

This is all an act.

It's killing him that his daughter is chained in a basement belonging to his demon ex-wife, and he is helpless to help her. He thinks he failed her. I also know he believes I failed him too.

"Let them go. You've made your point."

Gianna grins. "Your compassion was always your downfall,

bello mio."

"What do you want?" Aldo doesn't have time for small talk.

However, Gianna wants to gloat in her victory.

She walks toward us, her gaze bouncing between Bria and me. She's about to reveal truths that will destroy us all.

"I want what is rightfully mine. I helped build your empire, and in return, you discarded me once you got what you wanted. You used me."

Aldo shakes his head. "Still playing the victim card, I see. The lies you tell yourself, *amore mia.*"

The pet names they use for another are supposed to denote love, but they are anything but.

"I'm protecting what is mine, seeing as you allowed your love to blind you to what is under your nose."

Bria exhales, knowing her secret is about to be revealed.

"What are you talking about?"

Gianna looks at Bria. "Would you like to tell him? Or shall I?"

"Fuck you."

"What is she talking about?" Aldo questions Bria.

She lowers her chin, knowing what this will do to her father. "I'm the one who was stealing from you. I'm the one who was undercutting you."

Aldo stands tall, but the twitch in his jaw is his downfall.

"I'm sorry, Papa."

Aldo takes a moment and turns his attention to me. "You knew?"

I nod.

He shakes his head. "You allowed an innocent man to die when you knew the truth?"

"Yes."

There is no point sugarcoating anything. I will accept my punishment.

He begins to pace, needing a moment it seems to digest that the two people he trusted betrayed him.

"I was only trying to protect you," Gianna has the gall to say. "Your daughter's dealing affected us both. This is why I brought her here."

"Oh bull-fucking-shit! You only have your best interests at heart. You brought me here to blackmail my father!"

"Your father's loyalty has cost us both a lot of money. You undercut us both. Neither of you would have ever told him. I'm doing this for his own good."

"Enough," Aldo says, defeated.

His own flesh and blood betrayed him. There's no coming back from this.

"You think I'm unfit to run my empire, and you're the best candidate for the job?"

"Yes. I'm giving you a choice to hand it over to me, or I will take it from you. When word gets out that your own daughter betrayed you, your reputation will be ruined. I'm helping you save face."

We all know that's a load of shit. Gianna does everything to benefit herself. Her empire is in shambles, so she needs another to stabilize her failing kingdom. She hopes Aldo's slipup will sway his men into siding with her.

But they don't have a choice because there will only be one drug lord come morning.

Aldo sighs, twirling the ring on his pinkie. There's no way he will do what Gianna is proposing. But she also has him by the balls. This is a disgrace in the eyes of his men, and they would expect him to deal with Bria betraying him how he would if this were a stranger.

She is to be made an example of.

"Why did you do this? Did I not provide enough for you?"

Bria is quiet, but her trembling breaths reveal she's on the brink of tears. "It was about power," she confesses, as it seems the apple doesn't fall far from the tree. "I liked that my name instilled fear in others. Do you realize how hard it is being your daughter? I'm forever known as Aldo Cattaneo's daughter. Not Bria.

"This gave me my own identity. I was someone."

"*Bambina*, you were always someone. You were *my* someone. My world. Your mother didn't die—"

"Don't you dare!" Bria cries, yanking at the chains around

her wrists. "She is dead because of you! Because of your stupid drug wars!"

"Yet you follow down the same path as me. I do not understand any of this. I failed you. This is my punishment. And I accept."

"So choose," Gianna says, stepping forward and placing her palm on Aldo's cheek. "Your daughter or your kingdom. For you know, you cannot have both."

And she's right.

If Aldo wishes to continue being the top dog, Bria cannot live. It will show weakness. His men will eventually side with Gianna. But Gianna isn't patient. If he were to step down, Aldo's men would have no choice but to be loyal to Gianna, for these men have a taste for money and power. There's no way they would ever turn over a new leaf and walk away from this life of crime.

Aldo looks at me, and I suddenly feel guilty. Like I too betrayed my father. "What would you do if you were me?"

It's apparent our friendship runs both ways. I respect him, and he respects me. Because of that, he knows my answer.

Fight...

I would rather die fighting than surrender.

He nods, reading between the lines.

"Let them go, and I will agree to your terms," Aldo finally says, turning into Gianna's palm. "There was never really a choice, though, was there?"

Gianna leans forward, placing a soft kiss on his lips.

Aldo is rigid, but he accepts his fate.

The moment soon turns when Mario comes running down the stairs, Italian spilling from his lips frantically. When I hear Valentina's name, I tug so hard at the chains that I almost dislocate my arms.

Gianna's cool composure is shattered when Valentina walks down the stairs calmly. Her white gown is splattered in dried blood. Her hair is in two braids. My stomach drops.

"*Tesoro mio*, what have you done?"

My dark angel is no more. In her place lays a killer who wants more bloodshed. She's had a taste, and now, it'll never be enough.

"*Ciao*, Aldo."

Gianna pales when she too sees the change in Valentina. So this means that whatever Valentina did was of her own accord.

What the fuck is going on?

Before anyone can speak, a blaring siren accompanied by red flashing lights assaults us all, and my fight-or-flight instinct kicks in.

I don't know what's happening, but this moment will change history.

Mario pulls a gun on Aldo, but Valentina elbows him in the nose, disarming him. She reaches for the gun, and I wonder if she's had a change of heart. But when she points the gun at Aldo, I realize that she sees Aldo as her prey.

But why?

He ducks out of the way, but Gianna kicks Valentina's hand, causing the gun to fly.

More men come running down the stairs, their hysterical cries stating that the security system has been breached, and men swarm the grounds.

Gianna's perfect facade is fractured because this is do or die.

I don't understand whose side anyone is on. Why is Gianna disarming Valentina? But more importantly, why is Valentina trying to kill Aldo? She has only known him to be the man who was kind to her when no one was when she was a child.

Unless…

What the fuck has Gianna told her?

I yank furiously at the chains. I need to get free.

Aldo reaches for the discarded gun and runs to where I am, shooting the chains. The moment they snap, I run for Valentina, who is trying to get past Gianna. However, Gianna holds her back.

"Get out of the way!" Valentina screams, eyes wild as she stares at Aldo.

"What did you do?" Gianna asks, but she knows. Valentina's blood-soaked nightgown reveals that she finally got her revenge on Father Merry.

"Who saw you?" I push Gianna out of the way, shaking Valentina by her upper arms.

It's as if she finally realizes where she is.

Her eyes focus, and I see it—she realizes her vast mistake.

"You have to go!" I order, gripping her by the back of the neck and pressing our foreheads together. "You cannot stay here. Gianna can't save you from this. How could you be so stupid?"

"He needed to pay for what he did," she says, eyes frantic. "And so does he."

She yanks away, only to headbutt me and catch me unawares. Before I find my footing, she's running for Aldo, who is helping Bria to safety.

"Aldo!" I scream, warning him that Valentina is coming.

Gianna pushes past me, again attempting to stop Valentina. But nothing is stopping her.

She turns and kicks Gianna in the stomach. Gianna stumbles backward, stunned. This is the first time Valentina has disobeyed her.

Aldo's men cascade down the stairs, and it's war.

Men from opposing teams fight, the macabre scene heightened by the flashing red lights and the urgency of the shrill alarm.

Gianna smirks. She appears proud that Valentina is fighting

her. Has she been prepping us for this final showdown all along?

Aldo and Bria come to me. "Now is the time to take the bitch down!"

If that's Aldo's pep talk, then I'm sold. But on one condition—Valentina doesn't get hurt.

"I promise," Aldo says, reading my thoughts. "But do you know why she wants me dead?"

"No doubt some lie Gianna spun."

"We finish this."

Nodding, we go into battle, punching, kicking, and disarming Gianna's men. Picking up a fallen gun, I fight my way through the mayhem, saving my bullets for the woman who destroyed our lives. Gianna and Valentina are still fighting, and no matter how many times Gianna knocks her on her ass, Valentina always gets back up.

I want to believe she's fighting because she's finally seen Gianna for who she really is, but it's apparent Valentina's goal is to get to Aldo.

I punch some motherfucker in the face and use him as a shield as bullets are fired my way. No one's life is precious in battle. It's every man for himself. And that is why I aim for Gianna's head. I don't have a clear shot, as Valentina gets in the way each time I want to shoot.

She is bloody and beaten, but she won't give up.

Aldo slaps my arm down. "Not until she surrenders."

"You're fucking kidding me! We're in an all-out war, and you're worried about your reputation!"

"This will never stop!" He beseeches I see reason. "She must be made an example of!"

I soon realize what he means.

He wants to blame Gianna for the mole in the midst, saving Bria.

"There can only be one winner, Lennon. I prefer it is me. Don't you?"

He's the better of two evils. But why does Valentina want him dead? What did Gianna tell her?

But he's right.

I can ask questions later because now, this bitch is going to be put down.

We fight side by side, Gianna's men a laughingstock as they don't stand a chance. Valentina limps, clutching her side, but she never gives up. Gianna is scolding her in Italian to stop, but Valentina shakes her head.

"He's the reason I'm like this!" The back of her hand comes away bloody as she wipes her mouth. "He's the reason my mother left me there to rot!"

I have no idea what is happening or what she is saying, but I look at Aldo, who suddenly looks guilty.

"It's true?" I ask, punching anyone who dares interrupt this moment of truth.

"I can explain."

But it's too late.

"You knew this entire time, yet you never said a word."

"Lennon…"

I don't give him a chance to speak. I punch him straight in the jaw. He staggers back while Bria's eyes widen.

"What the fuck are you doing?"

I can't speak because I feel nothing but betrayal. I trusted him, but he's been lying to us both this entire time. He came to the orphanage to "rescue" Valentina, but he was only there to save his ass in case she ever found out the truth.

I always thought Gianna was the villain, but is Aldo the bigger monster of us all?

At this point, I don't trust anyone. All they care about is greed and power. I was wrong to ever doubt Valentina, and now I must right the wrongs.

"Lennon, don't be stupid!" Bria screams, but I ignore her and punch Aldo square in the jaw.

Aldo and I commence fighting while Gianna and Valentina are still locked in battle. I read Aldo's moves and dodge each attack with ease. Bria grips my forearm, attempting to stop me, but if she is against me, then she is the enemy too.

I don't want to hurt her, but if I have to choose, she will always lose.

Valentina is suddenly by my side and has no issues fighting

a girl. She kicks Bria in the stomach, who staggers backward, clutching her abdomen.

This is how I wanted this war to go—Valentina and I on the same side. We don't talk; we merely fight to protect the other because now, it really is us versus the world.

Valentina and I are shoulder to shoulder, so I assume she has knocked Bria out cold. We face off with Aldo, who stands before us, shaking his head.

"All I wanted was to help you."

"Don't fucking lie! Gianna told me the truth! You came to that orphanage because you felt guilty for everything you'd done. My mother—"

"I was saving you from your mother!" he interrupts, on guard.

"Liar! You said you wanted my fighting spirit. That you needed it to succeed. That I was invaluable to you. Remember? Why?"

When Aldo doesn't speak, Valentina steps forward and presses her gun to the middle of his forehead.

"You know why. You are the key to changing all of it."

"What does that mean? My mother hid away from you because she was scared of you. Why did you come to the orphanage? To kill me too?"

"Kill you? Your mother is alive. She is—"

"I know where she is! I've seen her. She's tied to a fucking bed, a medicated zombie, thanks to you!"

Confusion, followed by shock, passes over Aldo's face, and I see that he has no idea what she's talking about. It angers Valentina, and she cocks the trigger but never shoots because I disarm her.

She is stunned, but that soon turns to anger. "Lenny, get out of the way!"

I stand in front of Aldo, using my body as a human shield. "Stop, please, just for one minute. Tell me what Gianna has said."

I don't know who to believe. I need to hear all sides of the story because history has proven Gianna to be nothing but a liar. Aldo has been nothing but a friend. Nothing makes sense.

"You choose him over me?"

Gripping her cheeks, I beg she sees reason. "I always choose you, *tesoro mio*. But tell me why you want him dead."

"Gianna told me the truth, that Aldo was in love with my mother, he was obsessed with her. And to protect me, she left me at the orphanage. He would use me to find my mother because he's been looking for her for years. That is why Gianna trained us!

"To kill Aldo so my mother can be free."

"And Gianna gets his empire." I fill in the blanks.

"I saw her in some psych ward, Lenny! I cannot allow him to live! He destroyed her life and mine!"

This doesn't make any sense.

I turn to Aldo, who has heard every word.

He shakes his head. "How she lies. She will say anything to win. Think back to when I came for you. Did I ever frighten you? Yes, I came with an ulterior motive, but it is not what Gianna said.

"*Bellezza*, your mother is—"

A gunshot suddenly rings out…but it's not Valentina who shoots.

Aldo drops to the ground, his white shirt staining red.

Both Valentina and I gasp.

Gianna walks over, smoking gun in hand.

I can't believe my eyes. Aldo is bleeding and dying. He was about to say something Gianna didn't want us to hear.

On instinct, I run to his aid, pressing my hands over the wound to his chest. There's so much blood.

"We must go, *piccola*. The police will come for you. The sisters have alerted the police to what you have done. I cannot protect you here. Please."

"Valentina, no!" I scream, pressing harder down on the bloody wound. But it's in vain because Aldo will be dead in minutes. "She shot him before he could tell you the truth. You're nothing but a liar, Gianna!"

I can't believe I ever thought she could be good.

Sirens sound, and it's apparent the police have swarmed

the grounds. Men are dead and wounded, the sight a mass battlefield.

"Come with me," Valentina begs, dropping to her knees and grabbing my cheeks in her trembling palms.

"I cannot," I state because I chose a side—and it is not hers. "I won't entertain her any longer. I cannot save you if…you do not want to be saved."

Valentina's eyes fill with tears. "So now, we're enemies?"

I don't answer, and that is answer enough.

"You're choosing the wrong side."

"Well, I can't stay here."

"Because you wouldn't fucking listen to me! I told you Father Merry's day would come. But you just defy me. Over and over again. And now, look what you must do."

"I'm sorry," she whispers, and I know she means it.

But that doesn't mean she won't kill me if I stand in her way.

And the feeling is mutual.

I will get my revenge on Gianna.

One way or another, I will bury her for what she's done.

"We must go. Now!" Gianna says, tugging on Valentina's arm. If the police find her here, it's over for us all.

I look at Valentina and commit her to memory because I know the next time I see her, we will be hunting one another until one of us is dead.

"You're tearing out my fucking heart!"

"So this is goodbye?"

I ponder over her words. Among the bloodshed and murder, I say the only thing I can. "For what it's worth…I will never love anyone more than I love you. But love can't save us from what's fated in the stars. Run far away because when I find you…I'll never let you go."

She nods, understanding this for what it is. "*Ti amo sempre.* But love isn't enough. It never was. Goodbye, Lennon Shepherd. Let the best man win."

Gianna tugs her arm one last time, and she surrenders and leaves me—for good this time.

Every part of me demands I chase her, but that's all I've been doing and look where that has left me. Aldo wraps his cold fingers around my wrist and coaxes me down so he can whisper his dying words into my ear.

With his last breath, he changes my life forever, and I will never be the same.

Time stands still…

Bria's scream is the first sound I hear reborn as she throws herself onto her father's cooling corpse. Aldo's men stop and look at me, unsure what to do.

With the police hot on our asses, I stand to face the men, covered in Aldo's blood. "I'm Lennon Shepherd. Your new leader. Aldo is dead. We avenge him and the wrongdoings that were done here today.

"His death will not be in vain. He was a righteous leader. He sacrificed his life for his legacy to be protected. But none of you can be trusted. Gianna was the one who was working with his men to take down his empire. You need to prove your worth to me. To us."

Bria is the rightful heir to Aldo's legacy. But she can't do this alone because no one knows Gianna and Valentina better than I do.

My white lie saves Bria. But that doesn't console her because her father is no more.

The men listen intently because it seems they need a leader, and that leader is me. "We have a new objective. We destroy Gianna's empire, and then…we destroy her. We do not cower in fear! We kill anyone who stands in our way, and so help me God, if any of you betray me…I will destroy everything you care about and make you watch. Pledge your loyalty, your life to me, here, now, or leave. This is your one and final chance because there's no going back."

This comes easy to me because Gianna raised me for this. She just thought I would be fighting for her side.

The testosterone is suffocating as the men holler in unison, celebrating me as their new leader.

"Go, now, and we meet tomorrow. For those who survive the night, you are worthy to fight for me. For those who do not, may God have mercy on your soul."

With my pep talk over, the men scurry into the night.

But Bria peers up from where she cradles her father, blood mixed with tears. "What did he say to you?"

That is a secret I cannot ever tell. Aldo was guarding that truth for a reason, and that reason is now. *This* is what Gianna was protecting. *This* is her Achilles' heel.

"You will get your revenge, I promise you. But now, we must go."

She looks at her father, tears streaming down her cheeks.

I do not feel her pain because I need to switch off my humanity to survive.

"Don't let his death be in vain. Fight with me. We kill anyone who stands in our way."

"Anyone?" she asks, narrowing her eyes.

I nod, granting her permission to kill Valentina if she gets the chance. But she will never win against Valentina.

Bria lays a kiss on her father's forehead before accepting my hand.

I lead the way to freedom with Bria by my side, for Valentina has made a new enemy, and Bria won't stop until she avenges her father.

We flee into the night, too many of us for the police to apprehend, but before I leave, I set the basement alight and watch from the bordering forest as my once home burns.

I have a new purpose in life now.

I will get my brother clean.

I will run Aldo's empire with Bria by my side.

But most of all, I will never forget Aldo's dying words.

"Her mother is…Gianna. Gianna is Valentina's mother."

He perished before he could tell me more. But my need to kill Gianna only strengthens, and I will destroy anyone who stands in my way…even the woman I love.

Dio vi benedica.

Subscribe to my Newsletter: https://tinyurl.com/mvjjk6k2

Bad for You Playlist: https://tinyurl.com/bz438f82

ABOUT THE AUTHOR

Monica James spent her youth devouring the works of Anne Rice, William Shakespeare, and Emily Dickinson.

When she is not writing, Monica runs her own business, but she always finds a balance between the two. She enjoys writing twisted AF stories, hoping to terrify her readers...just a little.

She is a bestselling author in the U.S.A., Australia, Canada, France, Germany, Israel, and the U.K.

Monica James resides in Melbourne, Australia, with her Unicorn, and her three crazy cats. She is slightly obsessed with red lipstick, heels, and crime documentaries, and is *that* person who always runs late.

CONNECT WITH
MONICA JAMES

Website: authormonicajames.com

Facebook: facebook.com/authormonicajames

Twitter: twitter.com/monicajames81

Goodreads: goodreads.com/MonicaJames

Instagram: @authormonicajames

TikTok: @authormonicajames

BookBub: http://bit.ly/2E3eCIw

Amazon: https://amzn.to/2EWZSyS

Reader Group: http://bit.ly/2nUaRyi

Newsletter: https://tinyurl.com/mvjjk6k2

www.ingramcontent.com/pod-product-compliance
Lightning Source LLC
Chambersburg PA
CBHW070101120726
47909CB00002B/458